LIGHT OF EQUALITY

LIGHT OF EQUALITY

HAWTHORN ACADEMY BOOK FIVE

D.R. PERRY

DISRUPTIVE IMAGINATION

THE LIGHT OF EQUALITYTEAM

Thanks to our Beta Readers

Rachel Beckford and Mary Morris

Thanks to our JIT Readers

Veronica Stephan-Miller, Rachel Beckford, and Kerry Mortimer

Editor
SkyHunter Editing Team

LMBPN Publishing
PMB 196, 2540 South Maryland Pkwy
Las Vegas, NV 89109

Version 1.00, July 2021
(Previously published as a part of the megabook *Hawthorn Academy: Year Two*)
ebook ISBN: 978-1-64971-909-6
Print ISBN: 978-1-64971-910-2

CHAPTER ONE

"Help!"

A clatter of footsteps sounded in the hall before the speaker turned the corner, arms full of fluffy canine—his poodle familiar, Clementine.

"Darren?" I blinked.

His critter was in big trouble. Nurse Smith cleared his throat, raising his voice.

"Move! I've got an emergency here and need space."

We moved aside, Arick running out of the room and up the hall. Dorian stepped backward until he disappeared through the doorway. Logan and I remained front and center, in full view of the drama unfolding on the cot in front of us. The rest of the unbound critters crowded at our feet, herded beside us by Doris and Ember.

"Her pulse is high, too thready." The nurse looked up. "Did you find her like this?"

"She just collapsed after dropping a cup in the trash for me." Darren's voice quavered. "I don't know what did it. She hasn't been sick."

"Ezekiel!"

The vampire stepped through the door. He took one look at the dog on the cot, then leaned forward, wafting air toward his face and inhaling through his nose.

"She's been poisoned. Neurotoxin."

Behind me, Lena gasped and sniffled.

"Neurotoxin?" My nostrils flared, red tinting the edges of my vision. I knew a magus on campus who wielded that substance: Alex Onassis. My throat choked with anger, and I could say nothing more. The air around me began heating rapidly.

That's right. Get fired up and then find him. Make him pay.

I almost gave in because familiar-based magi had a code. Familiars were off-limits, always. Attacking someone's critter was a heinous act, like harming an infant. I lifted my foot and switched my breathing pattern to suit a sprint, but before I could take off, cold fingers interlaced with my blazing ones.

I looked to my left, expecting to see Dorian. He was an ice magus, after all, and had been nearby last time I checked. But it wasn't the new kid holding my hand. It wasn't even Logan, who'd used his water magic to counter my fire before.

"Chill. You've got to cool it, Aliyah."

"Dylan?" Logan named my savior. He stared down at our hands, blinking. When I copied him, everything looked normal.

"Yeah. It happened in the café. I followed Darren."

I shivered because Dylan's grip on my hand was colder than his air magic, which usually mirrored ambient temperature. The involuntary movement shook me out of my anger, and Dylan's grasp too.

"Administering antidote." Nurse Smith snagged the syringe off a tray Ezekiel held out toward him. "Darren, you have to keep calm. Hold her down."

"Okay."

But he couldn't. Darren trembled, his grip too loose. He paled and doubled over, holding his stomach. Was he picking up on her symptoms? Clementine flailed, nearly bucking off the cot in the grip of a seizure.

I rushed around to the other side of the dog, Ember swooping down in tandem. She dived to the opposite side of the cot, leaning against the poodle's hindquarters before she could fall off. I reached out, grabbing Clementine by the scruff of the neck with one hand and blocking her back with my other shoulder. After that, I locked an arm around her, pinning her to the cot on her side.

"Antidote incoming." Nurse Smith worked quickly, taking the dog's front paw in his hand and giving the injection with a grace I hadn't imagined he possessed.

She whined, crying and straining against my grasp. Darren, now definitely affected by his familiar's dire state, reached toward her face. Her teeth clicked together, jaw clenching and eyes rolling. He pulled back just in time. The impact of this entire ordeal felled him, and he collapsed into the nearest chair, slumping over and dry-heaving.

Dylan, always quick to respond to rogue bodily functions due to his time in food service, placed a wastebasket under the ailing magus.

"Will she be okay?" Dorian asked.

"I don't know." Nurse Smith shook his head, his forehead a tangle of furrows. "She's not improving as expected."

"This antidote is supposed to react with great alacrity." Ezekiel shook his head. "In magi. But neither of us are experts in extraveterinary medicine."

"Call my grandma."

"The headmaster's already on it." Dylan nodded. "He saw the whole thing upstairs. We just have to wait for her to get here."

Bubbe showed up with one of her levitating animal crates that transported heavier critters too sick to walk. When she was ready to leave, Darren followed, shakily leaning on her arm. Headmaster Hawkins stood by and waited for them to depart.

"I'll want a statement from you, Mr. Kahn, including a list of everyone in the café leading up to this incident."

"I'll talk to my boss. She was manning the counter too." Dylan nodded. "I should get back up there to finish my shift."

"No, I've closed the café down for now." The headmaster sighed. "It shall remain out of commission until it's been swept for evidence and thoroughly sanitized."

"You don't think it was something in the food or drink?" Nurse Smith asked.

"I've yet to rule that out." He sighed again. "But I hope not."

"Mr. Brown said it's a neurotoxin." I raised an eyebrow, taking a deep breath as I went ahead, damned the torpedoes, and stood up to the headmaster. "I hope accidental contamination isn't all you're ruling out, sir."

"My investigation's details are on a need-to-know basis. You, Miss Morgenstern, do not need to know."

"What about me?" Hal stood in the doorway, clinging to Faith's arm.

"No."

"You're the headmaster." Hal narrowed his eyes. "Sir."

I wondered what that exchange was about, but didn't get a chance to ask.

"Everybody out of my infirmary." Nurse Smith waved his hands in a shooing gesture that didn't include Hal's father.

Even Zeke filed into the hallway with us, heading up the ramp and into the lobby. He turned down the corridor beside the stairs toward the takeout window. The vampire CNA was friends with Penelope but didn't much like mingling with the rest of the students. I couldn't blame him, with anti-vampire sentiment rampant on campus.

When I turned, I noticed Dorian was nowhere to be found. He'd either faded into the crowd of students milling about socializing or had headed up the stairs without saying goodbye. I asked where he went, but Dylan and Logan didn't know. Lena stood nearby, back pressed against the wall, shrugging.

"Dinner?" I jerked my thumb at the cafeteria, including the shy girl in my question. She shook her head and made a beeline for the stairs.

"I'm not hungry after all that." Logan sighed. "I'm going upstairs to hit the books, and maybe the showers. See you tomorrow."

"I'm not hungry either, but I could use a cuppa." Dylan beckoned, sauntering toward the cafeteria. "Come on."

Once we were seated with tea and toast, which I insisted Dylan include, I asked him the million-dollar question.

"What's with the super-chilled air?"

"I don't know, but I'm worried it's the good old E-word."

"You need to do something about that right away." I picked up my tea to keep from fidgeting. The idea that Dylan might also be an extra-magus had me on edge for reasons I couldn't define. "If last year taught me anything, it was to ask for help. The headmaster said I should have gone to Luciano about it."

And you're still not telling anyone about me, or asking your crush whether he's got a devil on his shoulder. How interesting.

"Don't worry, I'll learn from your mistake. Watch."

He pulled out his notebook from the lecture, the one that transcribed everything off the magical blackboards. These worked two ways, letting us ask teachers questions outside class by writing them in the book.

"Do you have a pen?"

"Sure." I pulled one from behind my ear and set it on the table. I didn't want our hands touching again, especially not when he could see my face.

"Thanks."

I watched him print out words requesting a meeting with Professor DeBeer immediately. The words faded, typical when the recipient saw the message. A new one appeared briefly, instructing him to report to her office in twenty minutes. At least he'd have time to finish his toast and tea.

"I'm going to nip this in the bud." He grinned. "No secrets, no lies."

"Good." I held the teacup in front of half my face, hoping to hide any awkward expression that might cross it. "Make sure you say the E-word right away. That was my mistake, not telling anybody."

"Well, you've got Luciano, so I can barely blame you. He's not an approachable fellow."

"You'd be surprised if you were in his class. He looks and sounds stodgy, but underneath it all, he's a big softie."

5

"How?" Dylan's eyes narrowed. "He's a poison magus. Don't you suspect him? You know, about Clementine?"

"No way." I shook my head. "He taught for decades overseas in very exclusive schools. If he were the type of guy to do stuff like that, his career would've ended ages ago."

"Fair enough." Dylan chewed on a triangle of toast. "But he was in the café right before it happened."

"That doesn't mean anything. Darren mentioned the trash can. I'm surprised the headmaster only asked for a list of people. Familiars have their own powers, and some are natural enemies. Bubbe uses herbs and light or sound to soothe them, but I haven't seen anything like that outside of the academic wing and the cafeteria. That's one reason we have Familiar Bonding, right?"

"Yeah. To make sure their bonds with magi tempers their instincts. I hadn't thought of that."

"Another thing. Those ties go both ways. Our critters influence us, too."

"I just can't imagine any familiar so bad they turn their magus evil. Gale keeps me company and helps just by being here. He's vain as a peacock but kind when it counts."

"Some people might use their familiar's instinct as an excuse for bad behavior. Or lean on their critters so much the bond goes sour."

"I know what you mean. Logan's family is a case in point." Dylan shook his head. "He lived with you for a week, so you know about their dysfunction. They're awful. I'd hoped they were the exception."

"According to Bubbe, they are. She says very few magi with familiars get as close as the Pierces to outright exploitation."

"I want to ask Logan how he's doing. His parents tossing him out, then calling the cops is madness. But I don't think he's ready to talk."

"It hasn't been that long. Just give him time." I shrugged, mostly at myself. Because there I sat, unable to take my own advice.

"Yeah." Dylan swallowed, then looked at me. "I'm sorry."

"Why?" I blinked.

"Because I feel like a whingy bastard." He stared at the dregs of his tea. "I'm supposed to make grades, become a doctor, and then make money, not talk about feelings. Or start writing poems and playing guitar badly. Noah didn't write that piece at Open Mic, I did."

"How many people love art, music, and books? It's all because of how those things make us feel. You went out on a limb, catching feelings and showing the world. That takes bravery, chutzpah. Don't put that guitar down just yet. You're not whiny, you just have a heart. I'm sorry for not reaching out sooner."

"I'll stop apologizing when you do."

"Something tells me the devil's throne will get encased in ice before that happens with either of you."

"Butt out, Spanos," Dylan snarled.

"I need to talk to Aliyah about—"

"Sod off!"

I blinked and shook my head, shocked, but maybe I shouldn't have been. The fuse on the powder keg between Dylan and Dorian had to run out sooner or later.

"Yeah, sure, fine, whatever." Dorian rolled his eyes, removed his hands from our table, and walked away, his back making way too straight a line.

"I can't stand that bloody fop." Dylan wrinkled his nose. "I don't know how you tolerate having him around all the time."

"Mostly for Logan." I shrugged. "He makes people laugh, at least."

"He's witty, I'll give him that. And well-dressed, thanks to wealthy parents. But his defining trait is laziness."

"What do you mean?"

"Dorian Spanos can't be bothered to participate in Gym. Has to have a doctor's note. In Creatives, he sat around the entire time watching Grace bust her ass at the sewing machine. And in the library, he sat in the corner conjuring lewd ice pictures on the wall where the Ashfords couldn't see. He's trouble."

"Well, I think Logan likes him. Likes-likes."

"Bollocks."

"The heart wants what it wants, Dylan." I gazed into my tea.

"Don't I know it." He crumbled the last of his toast into his empty cup, then put his plates together. "But mine's broken. Later, Aliyah."

He knows nothing about your *heart.*

I watched him leave, passing Tempe Fairbanks in the lobby on his way. She smirked at me and tapped her temple, then turned it in a slow circle beside her head. I rolled my eyes. She turned her back and followed Dylan.

So of course I rose from my seat and bolted toward the doorway, but by that time, both Tempe and Dylan had gone.

CHAPTER TWO

Dorian
Gryphon-Egg Problems

I couldn't handle watching the poodle and her magus. I know, I know. I'm a goth who sees beauty in darkness and knows death was change through tragedy. But I am also seventeen, and staring death in the face like this again would be too much, too soon.

That's why I ran away from my problems at Hawthorn Academy for the third time in as many days. I'm a coward, I admit it. I wouldn't be any good to my classmates and the new friends I'd made amongst them if the shit hit the fan courtesy of Temperance Fairbanks or anyone else, for that matter. They didn't know that about me yet, but eventually, they'd figure it out.

Yesterday, I would have told you my secret identity as a scaredy-cat was safe. Until the case of the poisoned poodle, I'd thought Grace was exaggerating, Faith had serious sibling rivalry, and Aliyah was a paranoid extramagus. The only one I trusted on campus was Logan Pierce, but he barely spoke about Tempe in particular or magisu-premacists on campus in general. His main concern was his family, and I didn't blame him.

It's ironic that my own folks accepted me no matter what, not that I didn't need it, all things considered. Ironic and lucky, I guess. I was secretly a unicorn in more ways than one. Anyway, Logan's home life sounded like a horror show, and I was worried about Parent's Night for his sake.

But I digress. That happens to me a lot. I don't know whether it's cowardice or laziness, but I'm all talk and no action. Changing the subject is safest most of the time, but it flies like a hardboiled egg in emergencies. Everyone and Aliyah's actual grandma wanted to act right then, which was why I ran off to find a place to hide.

At the top of the ramp coming up from the infirmary, I saw food service staff with protective aprons, goggles, and gloves on, closing off the café. Even that sadistic Coach Pickman helped. I couldn't hide in there, and I wouldn't want to for fear of neurotoxin contamination, but I needed a place to calm down with Mercy, who I'd tucked under my arm inside my blazer.

The library was closed, and the cafeteria bustled like downtown Providence during WaterFire. I would've gone to my room, but Eston was there with Kitty, plotting their Truncheons and Flagons adventures. Or enjoying some other form of alone-time.

I backed up, trying to remember Logan's descriptions during our campus tour. My brain kept firing blanks, not coming up with anything. Logan liked his quiet time, but probably managed most of it in his room since Dylan worked so much. I couldn't remember him mentioning any safe haven on campus besides the Café de Poison.

I glanced around the lobby, noting that the exit to the outer hallway was blocked by an enormous cleaning cart. Nowhere was left but the academic wing. When I got to the double doors with their stained-glass mural, my plan was foiled. The doors refused to budge when I pushed on them.

"Caw!" Mercy wrangled her way free of my blazer, swooping toward the doors. She wrapped her claws around the handles then flapped, throwing her weight backward.

I shook my head, sighing. "Out of the way, Mercy."

She cawed again and let go of the handle, allowing me to reach out and pull. The door opened, of course.

"Not just a coward, but an idiot too."

I stepped through the doorway to find the hall dark, though it wasn't pitch-black as I'd feared. The magical light fixtures gave off a dim glow, like dark mode on a phone.

I paced the hall, holding my forearm out in front of me to let Mercy perch there. She wasn't nearly as heavy as she looked because a gryphon's bones were hollow. That made them delicate, another reason for my caution since bonding with her. I reached out with my other hand and stroked the top of her head with my finger.

She leaned into my display of affection, as always. While walking, I relaxed into the unexpected quality time with my familiar and thought back to how I'd ended up with this adorably uncouth half-avian in the first place.

The Academy didn't allow pets, magical or not. They had wards to prevent all kinds of animals from congregating, mating, or giving birth on the premises, too. That is why I was stunned to see the large speckled egg in a shoebox outside my window one winter morning.

Calling what they have at the Academy windows was a gross understatement. They were small patches of wired glass, letting through only the dingiest version of sunlight. Sometimes I pretended to be a fish in winter, swimming under a thick layer of ice while I looked out the ersatz window in my dorm room.

Anyway, I had no idea what kind of egg it was, only that no animal had laid it there naturally. That meant a person had put it there, possibly a telekinetic psychic or a winged shifter. Magic didn't work on the interior or exterior walls at that school, including faerie glamour. The Academy was the closest thing extrahumans had to a military school in New England, and it was on near-constant lockdown.

I said my parents accepted me. I might have given the impression they were lenient, but that's been impossible for them over the last few years. I ended up at the Academy because I snuck out of the house after my sister went missing, doing that running thing toward where I thought Cassandra would be.

After a near-brush with a member of the Gitano Family, they sent me to the Academy for my own good. Dad never said it in so many words, but he was an empath, so I felt it. Mom might have had a vision. I wondered whether she saw me finding the egg, too.

No matter how it got to a windowsill on the fifth floor, I watched the egg every day. I knew it was magical after about a minute because I used the skills they taught magi in class and checked. It was blue and white, like my ice element. Maybe that was why I felt a connection, even though it was just this spotty oval on the other side of iron, wards, and glass.

Every morning I'd wake before inspection. Yes, they had that. Staff came in to check that our beds were made properly and the rooms tidy according to regulations. Anyway, before all that, I'd silently greet the egg. It turned into something like a ritual, checking the aura, seeing it pulse and glow brighter, like the baby growing inside it responded to a walking mess of a person like me who didn't know himself yet.

I took to caring about the mysterious egg more readily than any of the discipline exercises they made us do at the Academy. I peeked at it every night also, wishing her sweet dreams. Yes, even then, I knew the baby inside the egg was a girl. She told me, and I trusted without question. If only it was that easy for everyone else.

That year, I needed a friend badly. My roommate got sent to the Academy after putting another guy in the hospital. He called me sissy, a girl, and a whiny bitch, so I kept my head down. No jokes, nothing but deadpan compliance, worn like a mask.

The little life inside the egg made me feel connected, together with somebody in a way I hadn't felt since my sister went missing. She'd been seen with an older man in her sophomore year of college before vanishing. Out of this world, as it turned out.

They found her dead in the Under, aged an impossible number of years in a bargain with a Tsuchigomo—a sacrifice of life-force to the creature, payment to save the son she'd birthed there.

"Caw?" Mercy tilted her head, her inquisitive noises bringing me back to the present.

"What's up?"

She flapped her wings, pointing her beak at a room that turned out to be occupied. I heard muffled voices within. It looked like a classroom, not one for my year or maybe not any other. The academic wing had an awful lot of empty classrooms. I thought maybe listening in on someone else's drama might get my mind off my own problems.

I found myself hiding in the adjacent broom closet, index finger against the wall, using my ice magic to filter sound through the wood to assist in my eavesdropping. I'd learned that at the Academy, too, but spying was a self-taught skill.

"They'll never suspect it was us."

"Who's taking the rap, do you think?"

"Probably the wrong person. They'll question Onassis, of course."

"I'd make that mistake too. I hope you didn't make this puzzle too hard. You're a genius, even if none of them realize it."

"They'll get to it eventually, and then our hurdle will get canned. Probably lose his license, too."

"I still don't know why you have to get rid of him."

"He's a sympathizer, first of all. And second, he's protecting the biggest threats to the long game. Daddy said so."

"I don't get why, though."

"He's one of them, of course. Why else would I have asked you to pull his sealed record?"

"How did you open it?"

"I only peeked, and that's my little secret." The voice sighed. "But I can't show it to anyone else."

"Shouldn't we be trying to prove he's been lying instead of this frame job? A familiar got hurt."

"We can't prove that unless he reverts, which he won't; the conditions aren't likely for a withered old fool like him. Besides, Hawkins must know and just not care. This is better."

"What if you're wrong and he does revert? Won't they go easy on him, as they did on the Morgenstern girl?"

"I have a backup plan: an accusation to make. He'll still be removed from the equation, which will only help with the inferiors invading our campus."

"If Hiram were here, we'd never have to endure this whole degrading ordeal."

"True, but we also wouldn't have the opportunity to teach the inferiors a lesson right here on this campus."

"Point, set, match."

"I love it when you talk sporty to me. Come here."

Okay, so I'm a bit shady. I've listened in on all kinds of back-alley deals and clandestine meetings. I'm from a part of Providence owned by organized criminals. Being in the background of my family's dealings with them gave me a taste for selectively overhearing private matters, but I had zero interest in the carnal activities of a couple of bigots.

That's right, I'd just listened in on a conversation between magisupremacists, which my parents had been assured weren't tolerated on this campus. I removed my finger from the wall like it had suddenly heated to the temperature of boiling oil. After that, I extricated myself from the broom closet as quietly as possible. The last thing I wanted was to get caught by that dastardly duo.

If I'd been Grace Dubois, I would've tried peeking through the window to discover the identity of the couple in the classroom. If I'd been Aliyah Morgenstern, I might have burst into the room, hands ablaze, and confronted them. Logan Pierce would have called in the authorities. But I was Dorian Spanos, consummate coward. I couldn't do any of that, even though Mercy took off from my arm and fluttered in that direction.

"We're out of here, come on," I mouthed. Mercy always understood me, even when I didn't include volume while talking to her. Gryphons have amazing hearing, which explained how she heard me in the egg in the box on the windowsill through that magically warded glass.

She followed me because familiar bonds were stronger than anything in either world. And coincidence, the truth behind the myth of fate, warped and weakened even the most ironclad rules and regulations turned against it. The connections we made with others, when true and from the heart, could overcome almost anything, even a psyche full of fear like mine.

One warm spring morning at the Academy, something was wrong with Mercy's prenatal aura. When I realized she couldn't get out of her egg, I acted immediately. My roommate woke blearily, unwilling or unable to fathom my anguish over an egg on a windowsill.

I reached a hand out and pressed it to the glass, summoning all my strength and focusing on lowering its temperature as much as possible. The wards should've prevented this. They probably would have if I wasn't so desperate and hadn't also felt a fear that mirrored my own from the other side. It pushed my conjuring power to heights I'd never even heard of, let alone felt before.

The egg stopped rocking back and forth, as it had been for the last few minutes while Mercy failed at breaking out of it. I sensed her in there, stilling physically to muster her magic. Her efforts were downright Herculean, heroic in a way I never imagined anyone who cared for me could be.

In that utilitarian cinderblock room, I screamed without thinking, without stopping to adjust my pitch lower first. My voice went full soprano without cracking, but the glass did. That had little to do with the sound coming from my mouth, though. It was mostly ice, a deep arctic freeze.

And then the crack imploded, shards of metal-laced glass flying inward through the window. My hair took on a grainy feeling like I'd laid in sand at the beach, and a patter like hail falling on a frozen pond sounded behind me. My face was wet in spots but with blood, not tears. Coincidence was on our side. Mercy and I were destined to save each other.

I reached through the small opening in the wall. If I'd been thinking I wouldn't have. I would've feared hurting my unhatched friend with my ice-rimed fingers.

But as it happened, the cold was exactly what Mercy needed to escape her egg. She'd been an ice gryphon all along, half-Arctic Fox and half-Arctic Tern. She hatched to the sound of the school's alarms blaring, and the first spoken words she heard outside the egg weren't mine but my horrible roommate's.

"Sissy's got a trash gryphon."

Before I could respond to his indignities, the door burst open. The Academy's brute squad dragged me off to the captain's office. Yes, they called the head of the Academy "the Captain."

They locked me in a room alone with Mercy until my parents showed up. Because they're amazing, that only took half an hour. Rhode Island is a small state, but they lived on the other side of two bridges from the Academy.

They home-schooled me for the last few weeks of that year, then pulled some strings and got me in at Hawthorn Academy on probation, but still an improvement in my academic life. My social one, too. Until the poisoning, anyway.

"Caw!" Mercy kept trying to fly toward the classroom, but I stood at the doors leading to the lobby already. I wasn't going, and my familiar knew it. I reached out and pushed the door, and she sailed through over my head. I would've walked in and mingled with the crowd in the lobby or the caf, but I couldn't yet. The experience alone in the academic wing had me too shaken up for that.

My sister had died because she knew too much and pushed too hard. She got caught up with the wrong guy, and he used her for his own ends. When she stood up to fight, they struck her down forever. I owed it to my parents and Mercy not to end up in the same situation. Maybe this time, instead of cowardice, running was the better part of valor.

I gazed at the stained-glass doors for a moment, trying to compose myself. The mural on them was titled Long Division, depicting a scene straight out of the Under. I couldn't stop the tears. I just couldn't handle it anymore—the stress of being in a new place with magi who had no idea what they might be in for.

My family had already lost enough to shifter crimelords and magisupremacists. Now here I was, trapped on a campus with more than one and no idea whether they were students, staff, or faculty— because I had run away.

I needed to talk to somebody, knowing that instinctively. Who could I trust? Obviously, the people I'd overheard were still in the academic wing. It'd be easy to jump to the conclusion that anyone out in the common areas right now wasn't them. But they couldn't be acting alone.

I wouldn't go to the headmaster because he'd start an investigation. The student handbook said that in cases of serious allegations, accusers couldn't remain anonymous. There was no way to be sure who at Hawthorn Academy was safe to talk to, except for the one person they'd mentioned.

Aliyah Morgenstern.

But when I found her in the cafeteria and tried approaching her, Dylan had nearly bit my head off. I left, heading into the hallway between the lobby and the school's entrance, which wasn't blocked anymore. I leaned against the wall, thinking about requesting to call my parents to ask if I could go home. Chickening out again.

"Caw." Mercy butted her head against my cheek. When she did that, an idea cracked through the heat of my panicked thoughts like an ice cube dropping into a fresh cup of coffee.

I could wait until October when the extramural guests arrived on campus. I'd definitely find allies against organized bigots amongst their ranks. Not all magi were magisupremacists, but all magisupremacists were magi. Other extrahumans could probably be trusted. In October, I could make psychic, shifter, and changeling connections, and then I'd have help with all this.

"I love you, Mercy." I stroked the fur on her hindquarters, and she curled her bushy tail around my wrist. "I don't know what I'd do without you."

CHAPTER THREE

Aliyah

At the end of dinner, Dylan headed toward the stairs. I couldn't handle any more socializing, but the café was shut down anyway, along with the lounge beside it. I wasn't sure what to do, so I paced around the lobby, trying to think of somewhere to be alone.

I walked down the hall toward Penelope's window, just to have room to stretch my legs without passersby looking at me. When I reached the end, I turned around and headed back. I thought about checking the gym, seeing if it was open. Maybe I could run some laps. But I remembered Coach Pickman saying it was being cleaned that night.

That left me no choice but to head toward the stairs. Maybe it'd be best to sleep off my bad mood. While dodging through the crowds of chattering groups in the open space, I kept my eyes down to avoid getting sucked into any conversations. That turned out to be a huge mistake.

My shoulder made contact with someone, and I looked up into the face of the last person I wanted to see.

Or maybe you do want to see him. Give him a piece of your mind, why don't you?

I typically didn't heed advice from the voice in my head because that way lay madness, but nothing about this entire day could reasonably be called sane. My mouth opened, spewing thoughts and opinions before I could stop their escape.

"How dare you!" I put my hands on my hips, glaring into Alex Onassis's eyes. "She's in intensive care, you asshole."

"What?" He blinked, taking a step back. His basilisk reared up on his shoulder, mimicking his movements.

"I understand you're no friend of Darren's, but hurting his poor innocent dog? That's beyond the pale, even for you."

"Clementine's in trouble?" His face paled and his jaw dropped. "I wouldn't hurt her in a million years."

"You expect me to believe that?" The right side of my mouth curled up in a sneer. "She was poisoned with neurotoxin, your specialty. I have direct and personal experience with that."

A gaggle of first-years stood transfixed by our confrontation, but I didn't care.

"I didn't!" He held a hand up to his cheek as though he'd been slapped. "I wouldn't poison someone's familiar. What kind of monster would do that?"

"You tried to whammy a sauna full of magi last semester." I snorted. "You wouldn't have stopped if I hadn't gotten in your way, either. I know you wouldn't think twice about it with other extrahumans."

"I'm not evil." He shook his head, the hand he'd held to his face before now trembling in front of it. "Familiars are off-limits. And we shouldn't be talking."

"It's true." Elanor Pierce sauntered over. "Pick your battles wisely, Aliyah. Your bully is showing."

"I'm not a bully." I blinked.

You could've fooled me.

"I'm not." I wrung my hands, focusing on Elanor instead of the voice. "But if you'd been in the infirmary, saw what happened, you might be asking the same questions."

"Not in that tone or in that state." Elanor raised her eyebrow, jerking her chin at my fists.

"Oh." I glanced down, seeing the glow around them. I hadn't set my blazer on fire; this was solar magic. All the same, my lack of self-control disturbed me. "Sorry."

"Is it true about Clementine?" Elanor crossed her arms over her chest, tilting her head. "Was she really poisoned?"

I nodded. "Nurse Smith called my grandmother in and everything."

"I gotta go check on Darren." Elanor dropped her arms. "If you guys have a knock-down drag-out, I'm reporting you both to the headmaster. You're both on probation. Stay civil or get the boot."

I put my hands behind my back, and Alex's shoulders eased. He took a deep breath, then let it out with a sigh, seeming to deflate. There was nothing quite like the threat of imminent expulsion to stop a fight at good old Hawthorn Academy.

"It wasn't me, I swear on all the gods of Olympus." He put his hand over his heart.

"Fine." I took a deep breath, trying to settle my agitation. "I believe you. About this."

"Thank the gods."

We stood in silence as the hushed group of students around us dispersed.

"Don't thank them just yet." I shook my head. "We're on opposite sides at this school. Clementine wasn't your fault, but somebody did this, and I'll find out who eventually. If your poison was involved in any way, even if someone stole it, I'll make sure everybody knows."

"So will I." He nodded. "Nobody steals from me and gets away with it, Aliyah. But I'm not the only poison magus on campus by a long shot."

"I know what you've been planning all summer." I turned my head, giving him side-eye to shame the devil. "I saw you last year, with Charity and that costume."

"What's that supposed to mean?" He stuck his nose in the air. It was a world of difference from how he'd reacted when I accused him of poisoning Clementine, so I knew he lied this time, but pressing further was too risky.

"Whatever." I shook my head. "I've got my eye on you, and Tempe too."

"Go write a Hallmark card or something, Goody Two-Shoes." He snorted. "She's not afraid of you."

"She should be." I turned on my heel and stalked toward the stairs, glancing over my shoulder to gift him with a withering glare. That should have been the end of the conversation, but Alex called after me, words that echoed in my ears, cementing themselves soundly enough to plague my dreams all that night.

"Nice talk." He raised his hand in a golf wave. "Your Uncle Richard would be proud."

My grandmother called on Darren the next day to give him a report about Clementine. She was on her way out while the second-years had lunch. Bubbe stopped by to say hello as I sat at the largest table in the cafeteria with everyone in my year. Even Dylan ate with us that time, though as far away from Dorian as possible.

After greeting my friends, she asked for a moment of my time. I got up, dropping my plates and tray at the dishwashing window before going into the lobby with her. Bubbe and I found seats on a bench near the double doors leading into the entrance hall.

"I'm not supposed to ask this according to the headmaster, but what happened to Clementine, Bubbe?"

"It was neurotoxin like Ezekiel said." She sighed, running a hand through her aquamarine hair. "If you hadn't helped hold her down for the nurse through that seizure, she might still be sick, or worse. I've sent samples to a lab in Boston, but so far, it looks like it had a non-magical vector."

She went on to explain that the poison might have been conjured by magic, but it had been delivered by putting it on a surface Clementine came into contact with. The lab results would do more to determine if the poison was magical or mundane in origin.

"Who uses poison magic mundanely at a magic school?" I blinked.

"Someone without poison magic, or any magic at all, who wants poison magi or critters like them to get the blame," she answered. "A poison magus covering their tracks is another possibility."

"The only person on campus without any magic is Ezekiel." I took a deep breath, trying to calm myself. "Some anti-vampire jerk could be trying to get him fired."

"I'm well aware, Bissel, but I won't say more until the lab work comes back." Bubbe put her hand over mine. "Except that I want you to be careful. Ember too. Remember that fire magic lets you burn poison out of yourself. If you have any friends with that element, you ought to show them how that works."

"So, you think we're not safe?" I blinked.

"I'm saying it's best to be prepared. I'm a medical professional, and it's something we learn over years of practice. So, perhaps mention it to your friend with the Sphinx, and Elanor Pierce as well."

"I'll do that, Bubbe. Thanks for the advice."

"Don't be a stranger this weekend, Bissel. I'll see you soon."

The rest of the week went by with little incident. Familiar Bonding continued with worksheets and magipsychic presentations given by Nurse Smith. The only interaction the first-years got with critters came from Doris and Ember making friends with Lena and Arick. She let Doris curl up in her lap while he practiced keeping his hands away from animal's faces and taking a few calming breaths before approaching them. I thought that by the next week, they'd both be able to continue the course as intended.

Lena seemed likely to find a magical companion, something sedate, but I wasn't sure Arick would ever bond with a familiar. He might be one of those rare students at Hawthorn Academy who ended up on the educational track like my mom. That would be a shame since he clearly loved animals with a passion.

Darren vanished from any social activity. We had a high tea, a study group, and a movie night that first week, but he attended none of those. The only time I saw him was on the way in and out of the cafeteria, and he rebuffed all my efforts at checking on him. I did see him whispering with Elanor in the hall between classes, so at least he talked to someone.

I decided to take Bubbe's advice and help my fire magus friends learn to counter poison. Kitty was easy to find, so I started with her. She ran her weekly Truncheons and Flagons game on Wednesdays, so I dropped by her room after it let out and Faith was on her way to the baths for her swim.

"I never tried burning poison out. Is there anything on the subject at the library?" she asked.

"Yes. I found descriptions in this book about Bishop's Row." I jotted the title down on a piece of paper for her. "We can practice together if you want. No poison's required for that, thank goodness, but it's easy to run out of energy, so we should have our familiars nearby."

"Can we give it a go now?"

"I guess."

The basic principle was something like having a fever, except induced and controlled by magic. We both conjured fire, and then I showed her how to focus it inward. By the time Faith returned from the baths, we sat flushed and panting at the round table in the middle of the room, our familiars snoring on the table between us.

"That was like a hot yoga workout." Kitty laughed. "Whew!"

"What was?" Faith raised an eyebrow.

"Some fire magic stuff." I yawned, too tired to think about anything but sleep. We said goodbye and I left for my own room, letting Kitty explain the exercise.

I tried to look forward to the weekend. I'd go home on Saturday and meet with Izzy and Cadence to chill out from all the school stress. Plenty of my classmates needed a break, and I tried encouraging them to join in. It wasn't easy, considering nobody seemed inclined to come into town with me.

Dylan insisted on sticking around campus with his guitar. I said we wouldn't mind if he brought it along, but apparently, he wanted to practice with some other folks. My momentary flash of jealousy cooled when he explained Elanor was looking for a guitarist to join a musical act in the extramural talent show.

Faith and Hal were heading into Boston for a visit with his doctor. They'd leave on Friday during Familiar Bonding, so I couldn't even see them off. Grace planned to spend all weekend in Creatives, working on a project she insisted on keeping secret. And Dorian had to do homework and help Nurse Smith clean the infirmary, an ongoing task since Mercy had trashed the place that first afternoon in Familiar Bonding.

Finally, I tried to coax Logan into town, asking him if he'd visit Bubbe at least, but he said he wanted to help Dorian catch up on last year's critter-specific material. I couldn't argue with his insistence on encouraging good study habits.

Logan's academic strategies had propelled him to top of the class last year, so who was I to criticize? He was probably still worried about his parents, too, so I gave up. On Friday night, I hung out with Grace. Over chips and salsa, the subject of Logan's crush on Dorian came up. She wasn't surprised.

"Maybe they'll get together someday." She grinned at my blink. "You know Dorian's bi, right?" Grace shrugged at my dropped jaw. "We discussed it on the first day. We're only together for show, temporarily. He gets to skip the whole newcomer garbage and I get to look strong, keeping the rebellious guy in check. Exponential cool factor that makes up for no longer dating the athletic class clown."

"Oh." I looked away, avoiding giving voice to the first thought that popped into my head. "Why temporarily?"

"Because Dorian's helping me cement popularity with Hawthorn students. He won't go over well with psychics, shifters, and changelings, though, so I'll need to be single and eligible in October when the competing students get here. Then I'll play the field."

"Everybody in town loves Dylan, though. Cadence and Izzy do, and they're popular at their schools already."

"Why didn't I just stay with Dylan then?" She sighed. "Isn't that what you want to know?"

"You told me already. Too much emotion, right?"

"Not from him." She rolled her eyes, chagrin morphing to anger. "How can you be in love and not have sex?"

"That makes no sense." My face felt nearly feverish. I'd always imagined true love not requiring all the messy-seeming naked body stuff, or only exploring once you had a long history of devotion and trust. I couldn't imagine what it felt like, desire for the sake of it, but she took my words differently than I'd intended them.

"Right!" Grace's nod was as emphatic as applause. "I'd rather get stuck being celibate with someone I don't want to bang all the time."

I didn't contradict her because we'd end up in an argument about a subject I found utterly baffling. I had no time or energy for that. Instead, I got ready for bed. Spending the weekend coordinating events with Izzy and Cadence might end up as an exercise in cat-herding anyway.

CHAPTER FOUR

"We got the same list of projects." Izzy nodded. " I singled that one out too. Mostly because of you, Cadence."

"Me?" Cadence batted her eyelids, smiling. "Oh, you shouldn't have, Iz."

"You know practically everyone at Gallows Hill. Who's going to help most with this experiment? And will they be participating in extramurals?"

"Let's see. What kind of shifters do you need again?" Cadence raised her eyebrow.

"You can't tell by looking at this description?" Izzy tapped the paper, her eyes widening. "Have you been asleep in class?"

"Don't get on my case. I do a lot of work at school. And I've always been a little scatterbrained, you know that." I didn't like how strident Cadence's voice sounded while she was defending herself.

"I can always invite Azrael over and ask him." I shook my head. "Or we could just tell Cadence what we're looking for. Let's all chill out. We've got this."

"I don't need a lecture, Aliyah." Izzy's jaw clenched, eyes too shiny.

"Sorry, I didn't mean it to come across that way." I reached out, putting my hand over hers. "Are you okay?"

"I might not even have a spot on the extramural team." Izzy's lower lip trembled. "After I worked so hard last year."

"What happened?"

"Everyone at Messing is fickle. It's hard to describe, so I won't. I'll just give you a name." She took a deep breath, steadying her hands and her voice. "Jonah Arnold."

The name meant nothing to me, but it did to Cadence. She gaped like a, well, fish.

"No. Way. How did he get into your school? He's a vampire."

"Messing Academy admits psychic vampires as long as their years of existence total eighteen or less. Jonah's clairvoyant just like me, uses tarot cards and everything. Anyway, Dean Adelphi said he was automatically on the extramural team. That means I'm not going to make it."

"Doesn't Adelphi understand how much prejudice there is at Hawthorn against vampires?" I blinked. "Having him there is dangerous."

"That's why she's doing it." Izzy sighed. "Messing's its own counter-culture. Also, it's basic strategy. They're keeping redundancy to a minimum, like we're a Swiss Army Knife instead of a team."

"But aren't you, like, super-popular?" Cadence asked. "Isn't leadership important to Dean Adelphi's selection process?"

Izzy and I shook our heads at the same time. She jerked her chin at me, so I explained as best I could.

"Do you remember how Hal Hawkins was on my Bishop's Row team last year, just because he was the only space magus?"

"So it's nepotism?" Cadence narrowed her eyes. "Is Jonah related to the dean? Could you cry foul?"

"No and no."

"Is there any way you'd both be sure to go?" I tapped my pencil on the packet of experiments. "Magipsychic lab projects are a big deal, but that and Bishop's Row aren't all we've got going on."

"Maybe. Nobody's said anything official. I just overheard the dean talking to a teacher. She said he's our biggest asset." She patted the bag she always wore at her side to carry her cards.

"Got a weird feeling right after that, but didn't have time to do a draw."

"That tears it." I grinned. "The weird feeling could have been about Dean Adelphi's next hair appointment, for all we know. Let's make sure you're not redundant."

"Maybe."

"What extracurriculars are you doing?" Cadence flipped open a notebook and produced a pen with a downy black puff at the top. "If they're different from Jonah's, that'll help."

"We both play Bishop's Row." She shook her head. "He's a vampire. His reflexes and speed will get him on the team, no problem."

"What else?" Cadence wrote Bishop's Row, then moved her pen.

"Okay, fine. I'm in the chess club." Izzy rolled her eyes. "But he's the president."

"Okay." Cadence didn't bother writing that one down. "What else?"

"Ballroom dancing, which he got trophies for back in Chicago where he's from."

"So have you, in Boston!" Cadence dropped her pen and pad, clapping her hands and squealing. "Partner up with him for the talent show and boom, you're essential too."

"Cadence, you're a genius." Izzy leaned over and hugged her.

"You just told me I needed to study more." She giggled.

"Genius isn't just academics." I smiled, then rubbed my growling stomach. "I think it's pizza time, ladies. Let's head out and celebrate this stroke of brilliance at the Engine House."

My friends agreed, so we packed up our papers and notebooks, then headed into the early autumn day together.

"Bubbe?" I knocked on the rear door of her office, the one at the bottom of the back stairs. I'd just gotten back from my day out with Cadence and Izzy, and I'd promised to visit her this weekend.

"Just a moment, Bissel!" I heard her voice call from down the hall.

Her footsteps sounded solid and reassuring on the other side of the door as she approached and opened it. We smiled and hugged, then I followed her down the hall. She paused outside the entrance to the kitchen and turned to face me.

"Your friends are here, Harold Hawkins and Faith Fairbanks. They brought something I think you ought to see."

"Oh?" I blinked but nodded. "Okay."

She opened the door and I walked in, then sat across the table from Hal and Faith. Bubbe set an empty mug in front of me and poured red zinger tea from a pot. After that, she took her half-full beverage from the table and headed into the hall to do rounds for her boarders and patients. Mine was the only mug with steam rising from it, so they'd been there for a while.

"Hi, you guys." I wrapped my hands around the warm cup. "What's up?"

"Remember last year, before you righteously dumped the poisonous bastard?" Faith studied her nails.

"Yes, unfortunately." I nodded.

"You asked if his mother could look into Hal's family. Well, she did, but he waited until now to tell us about it. Anyway, he gave us this."

Faith pushed the piece of paper across the table toward me. I didn't look at it, at least not yet.

"Why are you showing me?"

"We thought you might have some idea what this means." Hal tapped a line at the bottom of the paper. "You're fanatical about the folks down at Providence Paranormal College."

"Oh. I'll help, I just didn't want to go poking around in your private stuff. Not after all the mistakes I made in that area last year."

"The mistakes turned out to be an advantage, though." Hal sighed. "Alex came through, but I can't get my brain around why."

"He sent it to us by way of Arick Magnuson, who positively quaked in his boat shoes." Faith rolled her eyes. "At least we've got one ally among the first-years. You made quite the impression on him in Familiar Bonding."

"I hope you're right." I sighed.

"The document seems to be in order, anyway." Hal tapped it again.

"But this bothers me. Something about it feels almost too familiar. Uncanny, even coincidental."

"All right, all right. I'm looking."

I held the paper up, reading the words printed on it. The document was brief, mostly a list of names with relationships to Hal's father.

"Gamila Haddad Hawkins is my grandmother. She made the stained glass mural on the doors to the academic wing." He shook his head. "I never met her, though. She's fae and went away for some reason. Business with a monarch, maybe?"

"I don't know. I only remember your dad saying his mother made that artwork."

"Let's stay focused on Stephanie's side of the family." Faith sniffed. "What there is of it."

"There's nothing here about her except that your mother's maiden name was Kiln." I tapped my temple, trying to remember. "And you're right, it rings a bell. Reminds me of something I heard, but it's off somehow."

"Absolutely." Hal nodded. "It's unique because everything on Dad's side is a birth or baptismal record, but hers is a GED record at North Shore Community College. She covered up being a dhampyr, but that can't be all."

"That name must be an alias." Faith said. "It makes sense, but if you're hiding your status, why do it with a name so odd it draws attention?"

"Because you aren't sure what your name is?" I shrugged. "Her kind were victims for ages, moved from one place to another and fed from. Maybe Kiln was the only name she could think of that wouldn't hurt anyone."

"My mom never had much empathy," Hal said, "And she's the opposite of genuine under the masks she wears in public. No, Aliyah. I can't afford to entertain the idea that she's somehow secretly sad. You never met her, so I don't blame you for misjudging her."

"Parents screw up." Faith put her arm around him, leaning his head on her shoulder. "They're flawed, they make mistakes. The really bad ones do horrifying shit on purpose, like sell their kids to the highest bidder, which is my guess about how she ended up here."

I couldn't say anything. My own folks were as close to perfect as you could get, despite my mom's estranged family. Anything I said would sound trite, so I looked at the paper again, trying to think of an alternate path to discovering Stephanie's true identity. My brain kept going back to Logan's parents and how they'd put out an Amber Alert to the police. That gave me an idea.

"Have you thought about missing person records? Cold cases?"

"No." Hal blinked. "I hadn't."

"I had." Faith sighed. "It takes a lot of in-person legwork all over New England. We'd have to hire someone for that. A private investigator."

"How much do you think it would cost?" Hal raised an eyebrow.

"No clue." I shrugged. "I don't know whether minors like us can legally hire them anyway, but it's something to look into."

"I'll check on it." Hal gave me a wan grin. "Thanks for brainstorming with us, Aliyah."

"I'd hardly call that a brainstorm, but you're welcome. I was wondering, what brought you here?"

"More vitamins for Nin and a checkup. Can you believe it's been almost six months since the last time?"

"Wow." I shook my head. "So much has happened since then."

"How's Dylan holding up, by the way?" Faith asked. "We've barely seen him since the beginning of the year."

"He's not doing so great. Feels left out of everything, mostly." I sighed. "At least he's got guitar."

"It must be even worse with the café closed. I heard about you confronting Alex the night it happened. Good job getting information out of him. Maybe that's why he finally gave the report to us."

"That's not why I did it. Total knee-jerk reaction. I'm kind of embarrassed." I let out a deflated little sigh. "At least I didn't light up the lobby in a bad way."

"I don't blame you one bit." Faith sniffed. "We still need to keep an eye on him. You know how Grace has our entire social structure planned out? You can be sure Tempe's got something similar going on, and if I were her, I'd counter you with Alex. You might have caught him off-guard that time, but be careful."

"I'm sorry, Faith." Hal shook his head. "You should be the one leading our crowd. You were born for this, but instead, you're stuck ushering me around."

"I wouldn't be anywhere but with you, and Grace is doing just fine." Faith squeezed his hand. "That girl has an uncanny knack for managing any task she puts her mind to. Besides, I like using my powers for good." She grinned.

"What did Grace say the first day? We're going to nice them to death?"

"It might not be that simple, but that's the idea, and I'm sticking to it." Hal nodded. "What did you say last year? Kindness is punk AF?"

We all laughed at that. Bubbe returned with Nin's vitamins to a room full of mirthful teenagers. I followed as we escorted Faith and Hal out the front door. After they left, I turned to my grandmother and hugged her.

"Bubbe, thank you."

"What for?"

"For being so kind to my friends. Helping us all. Going above and beyond. I appreciate it."

"Bissel, it's the least I can do. After we get to be a certain age, many adults think back to the teenage years, remember it as some golden age, but then we get even older and remember the rest. How hard it all was at the same time."

"There's something Logan says in Creatives: that it's almost impossible for something bright to stand out unless the background's darker. He's talking about art, I know, but isn't art like life?"

"And the other way around." She sighed, but the corners of her mouth turned up instead of down. "I know I already did my rounds, but would you like to have a look at our current guests?"

Of course I would. I followed my grandmother down the hall, filling the rest of my Saturday with the familiar but still fascinating task of helping around her office.

CHAPTER FIVE

Much like the previous year, the weeks went by in routine. Bubbe returned Clementine to campus on Monday at dinner time. I saw it happen; we had our take-out dinners adjacent to Darren. The lounge was cramped because only part of it had opened before the café, which remained closed.

Familiar Bonding proceeded, and we discovered Lena's element was poison. That shocked me. Shyness wasn't usually a personality trait amongst poison magi, and possums tended to avoid them, but she ended up bonding with the little marsupial despite all that.

Arick was a wood magus like Lee Young. He didn't find his familiar among the ones Nurse Smith presented, either. He bonded with one in the library, but not before he completely lost hope. I only saw it because I offered to return a book for Ezekiel.

"It's not going to happen, Mr. Ashford." Arick put his head down on the counter, something I'd never seen a student do in the library. "Is Academic as boring as they say?"

"Why not have a look at the introductory text, Arick?"

He pulled a large battered volume out from under the counter and set it beside the boy's head. It made a faint booming sound, but hollower than I would have expected from a tome that size. Arick stood up immediately, staring at the cover, which shook slightly before bouncing up and down.

"Oh, dear." Mr. Ashford took a step backward. "Cover your faces, students!"

As if in demonstration, he held his palms over his mouth and nose, like the masks carpenters wear to keep out wood shavings. Moments later, I copied him, rushing to Arick's side to encourage him to do the same. I knew what was coming.

The book's cover flipped open, letting out a voluminous cloud of papery dust. I squinted, wanting to see the critter emerge. I'd never watched one hatch before.

The pointy head looked more canine than reptilian, but that was because bookwyrms were chimera. It shook its mane out, sending up more dust, then yawned, revealing its froglike tongue. When it tried to climb out of the now-hollow tome its egg had been laid in, the poor creature succeeded but ended up falling headfirst off the counter.

"I got you!" Arick dropped to his knees, catching the critter in his hands.

Mr. Ashford lowered his hands, holding them to his heart and smiling. My mouth dropped open as I watched Arick stare into the bookwyrm's eyes. It let out a dusty croak.

"You're welcome, Skinner." He stood up absently, totally enthralled with the wingless critter perched in his hands.

"Your bookwyrm's name is Skinner?" I grinned. "Like the psychologist?"

"He hatched from an education textbook, so that makes sense," Mr. Ashford said.

"Well, it looks like you've got yourself a familiar, Arick." I grinned.

After that, he was all smiles. He waited with me as I returned the book, and I had the privilege of going with him to tell Nurse Smith the good news. Our remaining time in Familiar Bonding was spent on critter training and care, much to Dorian's relief. He and Mercy still needed practice.

Faith and Hal ended up asking Nurse Smith to conduct lessons in the same room as his infusions, mostly so they had company. He seemed slightly better, which was no small relief, especially with the specter of Parents' Night spooking Logan. He talked about it at breakfast one day.

"I don't know what to do, Aliyah." Logan shook his head, then gazed into his glass of juice. "They're going to show up. It's Elanor's last year. What if they try to take me home?"

"It's Massachusetts, and my mom knows all the laws, which are in your favor. She'll be here with Bubbe. They'll stick up for you."

"I can't shake the feeling that they're going to do something awful." He shuddered, almost knocking over his glass.

"I understand, mate." Dylan patted his shoulder. "This year has sucked so far, but once we're past Parents' Night, it's all fun stuff. Extramurals. Remember that? Maybe there's some good on the horizon."

"I guess so." Logan shrugged. "It's just, nobody else had their parents toss them out, then call the cops on them."

"You might be wrong about that." I waved a hand at the bustling cafeteria, thinking about my mom. "Maybe nobody here has been through that, but somewhere in the world, it probably happened before."

"I'm still scared. Can't help the feeling it'll go sideways no matter what I do. I know what you say about assumptions, so I guess I'm an ass."

"At least you're a smart ass, Logan." Dorian sauntered by with a tray full of empty plates. "I wouldn't be managing if it weren't for you, so at any rate, I'm glad you're here."

Logan stared at Dorian like he was a cooler full of ice-cold soda on a hundred-degree day at the beach. He strode by, seemingly oblivious to the attention.

"If I could only find a girl who looked at me the way you do at the Goth." Elanor appeared from somewhere behind me, shaking her head. "You've got it bad."

"No, I don't." Logan jerked his arm so hard he knocked over his juice.

It spilled across the table, splashing the remains of my breakfast sandwich in the process. I managed to avoid any of it dripping on me, thanks to Ember. She swooped down, flapping her wings to keep it from falling off the side like an orange waterfall. I tossed a stack of napkins on the liquid to soak up the deluge.

"Just say something to him already." Elanor sighed. "Do what you can about the stuff you have control over."

"Yeah, unlike your parents." Dylan rolled his eyes. "If you're going to give him sisterly advice, better to reassure him about that elephant in the room."

"I can't." She gazed at her shoes. "I'm not an insurance company, and they're practically acts of God. I'll distract them as much as I can." Elanor looked back up at Logan. "I wish they weren't giving you so much grief."

"Thanks, Elanor."

"For nothing." I finished mopping up the orange juice, dropping the sodden napkin on my tray.

"Whatever, Miss Healthy Normal Family." With that, Elanor flounced away.

"What did she just call me?" I blinked.

"It's several steps up from the crap Charity said about you last year." Dylan shrugged, then placed his hands on the table. The tips of his fingers paled slightly. "Anyway."

Something about his fingernails must've caught his attention because he studied them. He cleared his throat, opened his mouth, then closed it again. After another moment, he leaned back and shook his head. Whatever he was going to tell us remained a mystery.

"Aliyah, I wanted to ask." Logan started bussing the trays. "Will you go to the dance with me? As friends again, I mean. I just don't want to be there by myself, you know."

"Sure, Logan. At least none of us has to go with Alex Onassis."

We all laughed, Dylan somewhat flatly. It broke the tension enough to get us through that day, at least.

As the week wore on, I noticed Hal wasn't as late to class as he'd been at the end of last year. He came in just after the bell, a vast improvement. We partnered up in lab again while Faith headed Bailey off, leaving Dorian with Logan, who was responsible for him academically anyway. Matchmaking had everything to do with it since Faith and Hal noticed Logan's crush.

"You look way better." I waved a hand at his improved color and posture. "Is it the new treatments in Boston?"

"Partly, but Faith's been helping between classes. We meet at that stained glass mural and do the therapies Bubbe gave us last year." He recorded an observation about the fluid in the flask in front of us.

"Well, I'm glad that's working and that the doctors allow it."

"Me too. Who'd have thought the fact that she's an undeath magus would be so serendipitous."

"Coincidence." I smiled at my friend. "You guys are destined."

"I won't wager against you on that." He nodded back.

Neither of us said the obvious: that she was literally saving his life. I think he worried, wondered whether things between them were one-sided. From where I sat, it went both ways. Her family was so toxic it could give Alex's poison a run for its money.

I pondered my ex-boyfriend. Last year, he'd given Charity a vow to help with some heinous effort, but so far, he'd only denied poisoning Clementine and sent genealogy records to Hal. I couldn't allow his baffling behavior too much real estate in my mind. Faith was right; his mere presence could foil me by distraction if I wasn't careful.

Temperance was the definitive force in the social scene for first-years, and Alex was almost always on her arm. So far, it hadn't extended to us. Bailey hung out with the third-years. Elanor Pierce was their It Girl, and dating Alex had backfired because Noah hated him. Most of the third-years snubbed Tempe.

That left her with no choice but to set up a stationary orbit around Elanor's group in hopes of catching defectors before they switched allegiance to Grace. That vindicated her social strategy enough for my classmates to accept Dylan's misery as collateral damage.

Every Wednesday, the school cafeteria had high tea after Familiar

Bonding. The crowd around Grace grew, while Temperance's dwindled.

Arick Magnuson brought Giselle Ambersmith, who was his lab partner, to hang out the first week and introduced others each Wednesday. I kept my eye on the rest of the first-years every time because Alex had been sneaky last year, and I had no reason to think he'd changed.

If only I had more information. Bubbe was my only source, and she remained mum about the lab results. The headmaster continued working on the mystery. He'd sent a memo requesting staff and faculty to come forward with information but had let nothing else slip where Hal could hear or see it. Nurse Smith kept his lips zipped so tightly on the matter that he'd excluded Ezekiel.

The week before Parents' Night, Grace declared she needed me for some rounds through the dorm. She had me drag a canvas-covered wheeled rack up the stairs from Creatives and then along the third-floor hall. At first, I wasn't sure what she was up to, but after we knocked on Kitty's and Faith's door, I realized this was the result of her secret project.

Grace hadn't spent all summer just making clothes for herself. She'd made outfits for everyone in our year except Dorian, who she couldn't have planned for.

"Are you sure you don't have changelings in your family, Grace?" Kitty winked. "Because there's this total fairy godmother vibe going on right now."

"Nope." She shook her head. "A little dragon shifter way back on Mom's side is all. Otherwise, just magi. Anyway, do you like it?"

"It's so awesome, I can't even find words." Kitty held the red and orange dress up against her body. It looked like it was made of fire, flickering in the lights like a garment of flames.

"I never would've chosen something like this for myself, but I would've been wrong." Faith shook her head, holding the draped and flowing lavender gown with pale green and gold accents at arm's length and staring at it. "It's beautiful, a real work of art."

"Thanks." Grace blinked. She wasn't unaccustomed to praise, but

LIGHT OF EQUALITY

Faith gave it so rarely even I was surprised. "Come on, Aliyah. If we want to get this done before lights out, we've got to head to the next room."

"Can I go?" Faith asked. "It's Lee and Hal next, right?"

"Sure." Grace nodded.

Kitty went back in their room, and the three of us made our way down the hall to the next one. Lee answered the door when we knocked, then nodded and invited us in.

"You didn't have to, Grace." Hal shook his head, gazing down at the ensemble he'd laid out on his bed. The jacket and pants were black damask with a very subtle ram's head pattern, but the tie and vest matched Faith's color scheme.

"I wanted to."

"All the same, send me an invoice." He grinned. "Dad budgeted for my event attire this year, and if you don't, he'll head into town and buy something I don't like nearly as much."

"Me too." Lee stood in front of his mirror, holding his outfit up with the hanger under his chin. His suit was a deep earthy brown with a pine-green cravat that featured a glittering pin matching his signature purple bangs. He looked over his shoulder and grinned. "I was just going to wear my blazer. This is awesome."

"Do you have a date this year, Lee?" Faith raised her eyebrow.

"Maybe I'll bring someone, but only with the headmaster's permission."

"He'll say yes," Hal stated.

Before I could ask who Lee's mysterious date was, we headed out of the room and down the hall once again. This time, we stopped at Eston's and Dorian's room. Grace didn't have anything for Dorian because she hadn't met him until school started, but Eston was overjoyed to see the retro-styled powder-blue suit with its black cummerbund and bow tie. His shirt was ruffled and a darker blue like lapis lazuli, which matched his glasses.

Hailey and Bailey were utterly surprised to see us with the garment rack. Hailey's excitement was palpable, though her sister kept shooting the three of us suspicious glances. The garments weren't

41

anywhere near identical, despite the twins having the same build and coloring.

"I look like a unicorn!" Hailey giggled. Her dress was cocktail length, fun and cute with a kicky circle skirt in iridescent pink fabric. The entire dress had an ombre effect that reminded me of the sky at sunrise. Bailey's dress was a bias-cut maxi with a mermaid skirt. White rosettes that looked like cirrus clouds ran along the spaghetti straps, crisscrossing at the waist in front and trailing down the back of the sky blue gown.

Finally, we got to Dylan's and Logan's room, where Grace first produced a navy-blue suit with gold buttons and seafoam accessories. Logan oohed and ahhed over it while Dylan sat at his desk, emphatically jotting words down in his class notebook.

"Come away from that homework and check out your new duds."

"Really?" He turned his head and raised an eyebrow, his lip curling into a sneer. "You shouldn't have."

"I did for everybody else in our year. Last time I checked, you're still one of us." She shook her head. "Or maybe Aliyah wants to open hers next."

I peered at the rack. Sure enough, two garment bags still hung there. I reached out for the more voluminous one, figuring it had a dress inside instead of a suit. And I was right.

Last year I'd worn something from a mundane shop in Salem, and on Valentine's Day, Bubbe had lent me something magical from her days at Hawthorn. Both of them reminded me more of my fire magic than anything else. Grace had gone the other way with her creation for me.

As I unzipped the bag, hues of gold and pale yellow met my eyes. I'd never worn anything this shiny or light before, and it matched Great-Uncle Noah's necklace because the gold fabric had a sort of red iridescence to it as I tilted the dress on its hanger.

"You've really outdone yourself with this one, Grace." I took it from the rack and held it up under my chin.

"Whoa." Dylan dropped his pen. "You leveled up in sewing, Grace."

"So, are you going to open yours?" Grace tapped her foot. "It's almost lights out."

"I guess." Dylan paced across the room, stopping almost too short of the rack. But his arms made the distance. He snatched the garment bag off it, then went back across the room to stand in front of the mirror on his wardrobe.

Dylan's suit was off-white, bluish instead of beige. Like my dress, it was made from a fabric that changed color depending on how the light hit it. Pale blue flashed in the light, but on his suit, it made a pattern like clouds, or maybe white dunes. I couldn't quite decipher what she meant with the color choices. Everyone else's had something to do with their magical elements, but Dylan's didn't entirely remind me of air.

Does she know he's an extramagus? What's the latest news on that, anyway? He hardly seems like he's gotten help.

I didn't say anything. He'd scheduled that meeting with Professor DeBeer weeks ago, but there hadn't been an announcement or any other information publicly outing him like they had for me. Then again, I didn't know the standard school procedure for voluntarily reporting extramagi. I certainly hadn't followed it last year.

I wasn't in his class and had no idea what might have changed in there, but life on campus seemed harder for him instead of easier, as he'd hoped the day he'd told me about the ice magic. He had no obligation to include me, but it still didn't sit well. Izzy would definitely have flipped cards at that point, but she wasn't there, and I had no way to contact her until after Parents' Night.

Maybe the style choices did make sense without the extra information. Art was objective, so perhaps Grace's interpretation of air wasn't the same as mine. We were from different countries and cultures. Surely that explained it.

Or maybe not. Maybe your "good friend" Grace isn't what she seems.

I rolled my eyes at the Evil Inside Voice, but nobody noticed. They were all too caught up in the drama of Grace giving her ex-boyfriend attire for a dance she'd be attending with somebody else. I couldn't blame them.

As we walked back toward our rooms, Faith and Grace chattered about selecting makeup and jewelry after class during the week. I nodded, smiled, and contributed my opinions, but the strange encounter with Dylan stayed on my mind for most of the week, which made me feel like a bad friend. I should've paid more attention to Logan.

CHAPTER SIX

We had Bishop's Row tryouts the week before Parents' Night, too. I had so much on my mind, it felt like I was on autopilot through the exercises and trials. On Friday when I walked into the gym to read the list, I was shocked to find myself on the team playing mid with Dylan. Faith was on reserves with Lee. Noah stood at the board, smiling at the list.

"Alex didn't make it?" I blinked, taking a step back and bumping into someone behind me. We went down in a tangle of limbs on the floor, and when I partially recovered, I realized it was Faith.

"It's a good thing, too. Neither of us wants to be on any kind of Team Alex. He sucks."

"Not even all that well, according to rumor." Noah reached down, giving Faith a hand up. He left me on the floor, which I expected.

"Gross, Noah. So, are we talking again?" I stood up and straightened my blazer, crossing my arms over my chest. "We're both on the team."

"Only about Bishop's Row." Noah rolled his eyes.

"Fine." I dropped my arms to my sides and peered at the rest of the list. "But no more squicky locker room talk, okay?"

"Whatever. I'm surprised Grace isn't on here." Noah tapped the paper, which listed him as first defense. "She's better than you."

"Grace told Coach Pickman she didn't want to be on the team." I flipped a lock of hair over my shoulder. "Something about letting Dylan do what he's best at, and they still can't get along."

"They're exes, so things are going to be awkward." Noah rolled his eyes, then turned and began to saunter away. "Anyway, see you at practice, kids."

"Is he always like this?" Faith shook her head. "I wish they'd hurry up and chill out. Tempe's been way too quiet this month, and I don't like it. We'll want all hands on deck before extramurals."

"Agreed." I nodded. "Have you talked to him? I know you and Grace spent a lot of time together, but Dylan…well, you saw him with the suit. I'm not sure when he's going to get over it."

"Maybe Hal can ask." She sighed. "Not everyone gets past stuff by talking. I think he needs an outlet, like that open mic night but bigger. The extramural talent show might be the ticket, but it's months out."

"You're probably right." I sighed. "He mentioned practicing with Elanor once but never again after that. If only I knew someone else who was into performance art."

"You do." Faith's grin twisted into the shape I recognized is ironic. "But he's only agreed to talk about sports."

"Crap on a crap cracker." I closed my eyes. "Leave it to you to remind me about my own brother's passion for music."

"Well, it can't hurt to ask Elanor about Dylan." Faith tilted her head, her grin softening. "And you've got every excuse to meet with her, considering she's our team captain. I'll work on Noah."

That was the plan, but since Parents' Night loomed on the horizon the very next day, we didn't get a chance to have our chats before the big event.

Elanor was right. Her parents spent the entire school tour snubbing Logan in favor of her, so Bubbe let Logan escort her around, showing her the second-year set up in the lab, including the row of plants he had growing in the window there. Elanor hadn't brought Benny the philodendron, but Professor Luciano had gotten him a clipping from somewhere, along with rarer seeds, and encouraged him to turn the lab's window into a greenhouse. His entire face lit up, showing that off.

In Creatives, Grace beckoned us all over. She and Logan spent over ten minutes showing my grandmother the outfit sketches they'd designed together for Hawthorn Academy's cheer squad. They weren't as flashy as Cadence's at Gallows Hill, but the getups were stylish and flattering.

"What are you working on, Aliyah?" Dad asked.

"Mostly pottery, but here's something I'm carving from wood. Lee's giving me tips." I opened the cabinet where I stored my projects, producing the oblong chunk of wood I'd been working with. "It's really nothing much."

"I think I see it." Dad nodded sagely, taking the piece of wood for my hands. "There's the head, right? Is this Ember?"

"No, Dad, it's Gale." The clueless expression on his face prompted me to add more. "Dylan's dragonet. You know, my friend, the air magus?"

"Ah, yes. How's he been?"

"You ought to ask him yourself. His parents didn't show up again, and he's way more upset about it than he was last year."

Dad craned his neck, scanning the room. Once he spotted Dylan, he waved and smiled, then made a beeline toward the table where he sat with the guitar the library had loaned him long-term.

"It's nice of your parents, making rounds like that." Faith sniffed behind me.

I turned to see her dabbing the corner of one eye, then removing her hand in a flash before smudging her eye makeup. She blinked a few times, trying to let her expression fall back into resting neutral face without much success.

"Maybe because my mom had a hard time when she was here."

"You don't have to rub it in, Aliyah." She sniffed again, the redness of stifled tears fading from the tip of her nose.

"I'm not, and I'm sorry if it seemed that way." I wrung my hands, frustrated and unable to comfort her. "Anyway, where's Hal?"

"In the infirmary. With his father."

"Okay, then." I nodded, then offered her my arm. "Let's go find our critters and get ready for dancing."

"Together?" She blinked.

"Of course."

"You must have more important things to do."

"Friendship's important, so let's go." I grinned.

She gave me a lopsided one back, and we sauntered across the room. Faith might've showboated a bit, and I couldn't blame her. Her parents glanced up from where they sat with Temperance, examining some jewelry she'd made. They promptly turned their noses in the air and looked away. I understood how Faith might feel, even though my experience in being snubbed by family was limited to Noah. Dealing with one aloof brother had to be easier on the heart than an entire household.

When we found Ember and Seth, they'd been hanging around together. But Ember had dozed off, leaving Seth to prance back and forth in front of her whining, the nails on his paws clicking on the floor.

"Oh, Seth, honestly." Faith gave her familiar a soft smile. "Where do you get all your energy?"

I knew better than to try rousing Ember, so I scooped her up to drape her over my shoulders. She curled more tightly around them in her sleep, a habit she'd gotten into since this strange lethargic growth spurt had started.

"When will she get back to her lively self?" Faith raised an eyebrow.

"Bubbe says by November, most likely." I shrugged. "I miss her peeping at everything, but in a way, I'm glad she's been this drowsy while Mercy makes all the mischief."

We glanced across the room, spotting Dorian and his folks. They cooed over every little thing that had his name on it. He didn't bother introducing them to Grace, either. For her part, she kept her distance, and I hardly blamed her. She wasn't comfortable around parental figures on a good day, and she couldn't be happy about the lack of introductions. She seemed suspicious of how much Dorian's doted on him.

"Such a shame how his older sister died," Faith murmured.

"Really?" My footsteps paused. "I had no idea."

"I'm surprised, with the way you carried on last year about Providence Paranormal."

"I don't remember any ice magi in their pack."

"His sister was precognitive. Remember, he said they're all psychics in his family except for him. Anyway, her name was Cassandra, and she wasn't part of that aluminum foil group anyway."

"Tinfoil. And I remember now. She's the one the mob boss abducted." I winced. "How did you know?"

"Hal read his entrance essay, of course."

"Oh." I shook my head. "You know, I almost forgot he did that with all of us last year."

"A good thing, too. Everything might have gone sideways if he hadn't."

"Good point." I sighed. "And thanks for telling me about Dorian. The last thing I want to do is accidentally upset him by blathering on about my uncle."

"Don't mention it. It's all just part of our mutual crown-straightening society." Faith grinned.

———

Like last year, we made an entrance for the dance on Parents' Night in one big group. Hailey and Bailey even joined us this time, as well as Kitty and Eston, who hadn't before. Hailey had a surprise guest: Arick Magnuson.

"Temperance won't treat you kindly for this." Faith raised her eyebrow, looking at the shirt and tie he'd matched with his school blazer. "Honestly, asking someone in our year to the dance was a bad idea, Magnuson."

"He doesn't care, Faith." Hailey rolled her eyes. "Anyway, I asked him."

"Right." Arick nodded, smiling at Hailey. Skinner stuck his head out of Arick's pocket, crossing his eyes and sticking his tongue out.

"Whatever floats your boat, I guess." Faith said, clasping Hal's hand.

"First floor," Dorian called at the stairs.

A crowd of parents watched as the staircase moved us down. Expressions ranged from smiles to snorts of disdain, though most were neutral, which made sense. The majority of the parental figures here had nothing to do with us, after all.

Somehow, we were the first students down the stairs. We hadn't planned on that. In fact, Logan had wanted to avoid it. Without Elanor to run interference, his parents made a beeline for us. I escorted him toward my family, hoping the conflicting attitudes would cancel each other out, but of course, we got intercepted.

The Pierce boy can't avoid his family forever. You should know better.

"Good evening Mrs. Pierce." I put on my best smile, ignoring the Evil Inside Voice while extending my hand toward Logan's baffling mother. I'd had no interaction with her besides the strange video call at the beginning of summer. Her attitude and behavior had only confused me since then.

"You clean up more nicely than I expected, Miss Morgenstern." She tilted her head, giving me a once-over. "If only your parents would discipline you properly."

"I suppose the fact that I'm on probation isn't ideal. To you, anyway." I shrugged, allowing the Evil Inside Voice to come out for once. I figured its sass might counter her backhanded compliments better than I could on my own.

"Perhaps you'll be expelled, and my son can find more appropriate company to keep."

"You mean, like me?" Dylan sauntered over, hands in his pockets. Gale stood on his shoulder, glaring daggers at Mrs. Pierce.

"Ah, yes, the work-study kid." She sniffed. "Are you employed under the table somehow this year? It's the only way I can imagine you'd afford an outfit like that."

"Actually, our extremely talented classmate Grace Dubois spent the summer making attire for everyone in our year." I grinned, letting Logan raise his arm to turn me in a slow spin, the better to show off Grace's creation.

"Peep!" Ember swooped down from wherever she'd been stretching her wings, making as if to divebomb Mrs. Pierce before banking abruptly and landing on Logan's shoulder. She rubbed cheeks with him, then hopped over to perch on me.

"So, this is Logan's mother." The familiar voice came from behind me.

"Izzy?" I turned my head to find my psychic friend on the arm of Lee Young, which I would never have expected because Izzy shunned romance like some people avoid musical theater. Maybe she'd come with Lee platonically like I had with Logan. He'd mentioned bringing a friend, not a date.

"Hi." She smiled, but it didn't touch her eyes. I recognized that look. Mrs. Pierce was about to hear some inconvenient truths.

"Izzy, don't."

"Sorry, not sorry." Izzy reached into her beaded cross-body bag and pulled out one of her well-worn tarot cards. She held it up with the back to Mrs. Pierce, snorting before she flipped it around for everyone to see. "Ten of Pentacles reversed. Inauspicious to the max."

"I know what it means, you little charlatan." Mrs. Pierce narrowed her eyes. "I'm in total control of my life and need none of your nonsense."

"I flipped it for Logan." Izzy held her head high, basking in the disdainful gaze. "And thanks to you, he's not."

"This is the reason I didn't want him returning to Hawthorn Academy this year." Mrs. Pierce shook her head. "And why he'll be leaving with me at the end of the evening."

"I'm not going, Mom." Logan planted his feet, clinging to my arm. "I'm staying in school."

"Good luck staying on this campus all year." She stifled what I suspected was a fake yawn. "The moment you step off it, you're coming home."

"This is Massachusetts." The hand he had on my arm went clammy and cold. His voice cracked, but he managed one more defiant statement. "I know my rights."

"Then you'll spend the rest of *this* year here, languishing with misfits and miscreants. But *we're* not paying your tuition next year." Her smile reminded me of a steel trap. "You'll have to drop out."

"I can't believe what I'm hearing." Professor Luciano stunned us all by stepping forward. He snapped his fingers, and his strix familiar took off from his shoulder, silently gliding away. "My best student will have all the help he needs to complete his education. His GPA alone qualifies him for a scholarship I manage, to say nothing of all the volunteer tutoring he's been doing."

"My son *will* fail academically at some point. His grades *always* drop out, and eventually, so will he." She sniffed. "If he thinks otherwise, he must be as mad as that extramagus on his arm."

"If you can't discontinue abusing my students, I will ask Headmaster Hawkins to have you removed from campus."

"That's outrageous." Her smile reminded me of a barracuda's, but the figure that suddenly appeared beside her was a much bigger fish. "*My* husband's on the Board of Trustees."

"But you aren't." The headmaster approached. "Tone it down, or you'll be asked to leave campus for the remainder of the evening."

Her eyes widened, and her hands opened and closed rapidly. She said no more, just turned on her heel and marched back toward the stairs, where she waited for Elanor to descend. The headmaster nodded at Professor Luciano, then headed toward Hal.

"You shouldn't have challenged her, Professor." Logan stared at his shoes. "She'll find a way to get back at you, and you have enough to worry about."

"Nothing's more important than my students." Professor Luciano reached out, patting Logan's shoulder.

"What about your family?" Logan finally looked up, eyes too shiny.

"I'm an old man, Logan, and I never married. You students are the closest thing I've had to family in ages."

I noticed that the scene Mrs. Pierce had made had managed a feat Grace might not have achieved on her own that evening. It had distracted all the guests from Temperance's entrance with the other first-years. Elanor didn't make much of a spectacle on her way down the stairs, but that was clearly intentional.

The music started, the first song *Darkening of the Light* by Concrete Blonde. It was a throwback for sure, one of my dad's favorites from right before the Reveal. He said he found it oddly prophetic, a sentiment shared and often remarked on by Izzy's dad.

Izzy and I had spent a lot of time trying to decipher the meaning of the simple yet intense lyrics. The best we ever came up with was loss of some sort. We weren't sure what, though we always ruled out death. But now, watching Logan go through the process of losing his family, I began to understand, and I didn't blame him one bit for freezing in place as though rooted to the parquet floor.

How very appropriate. Why not just leave him there?

"No way, Logan. Let's show them how it's done." I escorted him to the dance floor, but by the time we got to its edge, his years of training took over, and he was the one leading.

The entire time we danced, he watched Dorian with Grace over my shoulder. I understood because my eyes remained on Dylan, who stood at the side alone, swaying to the music and tapping one long dusky finger on his shimmering jacket in time with the beat.

All of the Bishop's Row practice I'd done, along with Logan's cheer squad work, let us stay out on the floor for over an hour. He lost himself in the music, getting us through each song on autopilot. It reminded me of how I got running laps in the gym. At one point, I asked if he needed to take a break

"No, do you?"

"If you need to dance all night, I'm here for you."

He nodded, swallowing past some emotion I couldn't understand, but you didn't need to experience identical traumas to stand with a friend. I'd watched my parents do it my entire life without realizing it, so following their example came naturally.

Before the event ended, Dylan and Logan headed to the bathroom. I waited around, reluctant to leave them because the Fairbanks and the Onasseses loitered by the punch bowl. I tried not to snicker as I remembered the stunt we'd pulled last year, but it was impossible.

If only Hal Hawkins was strong enough to teleport something as small as a punch bowl upside-down over the heads of bad parents. I was certain about Mr. and Mrs. Fairbanks, but for all I knew, the Onassises weren't terrible people.

Don't be so naïve. What else explains their son's bad behavior?

"I don't know." I zipped my lips. I didn't intend to start answering the Evil Inside Voice aloud again, so I moved toward the wall, hugging it and staying in the shadows as I approached to do a little eaves-dropping.

"Can you believe it? A psychic at Parents' Night." Mr. Onassis snorted.

"They'll be all over the campus next week." Mrs. Fairbanks rolled her eyes. "Psychics aren't entirely objectionable, though inferior, but I shudder to think of our children on campus with undesirables like beasts and bloodsuckers."

I put my hand over my mouth to stop myself from saying anything. It was more important to listen right then, especially with the mystery of Clementine's poisoning still unsolved.

"I'd never have sent my only son here even though he bonded with a familiar if I'd known the extramurals would include subhumans." Mrs. Onassis sniffed, turning her nose up. So much for them not being terrible.

"Perhaps we should transfer our daughters to Trout down in Rhode Island." Mr. Fairbanks raised an eyebrow, tilting his head at his wife. "It would get our middle child away from that crippled boyfriend of hers."

Oh come on, say something already. Make a scene. It's your forte.

"Trout won't admit students with familiars." Mr. Onassis shook his head. "We already tried that with Alex. And besides, they admit even the savage changelings like redcaps and trolls."

"Perhaps with a large enough endowment, we could change their minds and policies."

"We made copious donations here before Hiram's son took over." Mrs. Onassis sighed. "My appointment as a Trustee was too recent to prevent this extramural nightmare."

"That gives me an idea." Mrs. Fairbanks' eyes glittered. "Let's discuss it over brunch tomorrow in town. The Lyceum, perhaps?"

"Why not discuss it now? I'd like to return to Greece as soon as possible. It's far too chilly in these northern climes for me." Mrs. Onassis pulled her embroidered shawl tightly around her shoulders.

"Too many eyes and ears here." Mr. Fairbanks made a show of looking bored, but he twisted a signet ring on his index finger, a nervous habit Faith shared.

"What's this?" Grace nudged me in the ribs.

"They're plotting something," I murmured.

"What now?"

"They're vague. We need to get off campus tomorrow to learn more."

"Understood."

The parents exchanged nods and smiles, then sauntered off. In their wake, Grace and I discussed our plan to discover theirs. Moments later, the boys returned from the restroom, and we gathered up at the base of the stairs, waiting for the rest of our friends.

I watched Lee escort Izzy to the exit, where they high-fived each other. Platonic, I thought, but Lee's gaze wasn't just on her face as he held the door for her. Izzy threw a wave over her head at the rest of us as she walked out, glancing over her shoulder at him one last time, smiling mischievously. Nobody else seemed to notice because they didn't know her as well as I did. It baffled me. If there was anything to it, Izzy would tell me in her own time.

We headed up the stairs together, some of us leaning on each other as we let the steps do the work for us. Everyone was tired from the stress of putting on a show for our parents and peers. At least one of our professors was on our side, and we'd managed to come together as a year, classmates working together for a common goal.

A feat we incorrectly thought would be no trouble to manage again.

CHAPTER SEVEN

We thought the plan was perfect. Grace, with help from Azrael, would disguise us to look like waitstaff at Lyceum. Dylan would distract management by inquiring about a job. Once there, Grace and I would make a show of bussing tables while eavesdropping.

You know what they say about the best-laid plans.

I tried to shake off the Evil Inside Voice, but it kept nagging me. Azrael and Grace combined Umbral magic and glamour like they'd done it a million times. Considering the amount of fabric they must've enchanted over the summer, that might only be slight hyperbole. Dylan stared into space the entire time, and I didn't blame him. Even I felt awkward watching that, and I hadn't been dumped by one of them.

"This will make us look like whoever a person most expects to see," Grace said after they finished. "But it doesn't affect us because we're in the know."

"Like Doctor Who's psychic paper?" Dylan smiled before he remembered who he was with.

"Dunno, never watched it." Grace shrugged.

"It's like Obfuscate in that vampire game." Azrael elbowed her. "Remember?"

"Oh, yeah, the one your cousin ran." Her cheeks got ruddier. Dylan pressed his lips into a thin straight line.

Control this situation before your plan floats face-down.

"That is like psychic paper, Grace." I rolled my eyes. "Maybe I'll throw a Whovian watch party over winter break. Anyway, we're on a mission, remember?"

We let Dylan go, waiting to walk past the restaurant's large window until he'd been inside for a count of thirty. That part worked, no problem. I thought we'd be fine even though the Evil Inside Voice insisted on reminding me that anything that can go wrong will go wrong, especially at the most upscale dining establishment in Salem.

And it did.

"Why aren't you girls out back prepping settings?" The woman glaring at us had a feral look in her eye, her stance predatory. I recognized her from around town and knew she was a wolf shifter who had run with the Tanks back when I was in elementary school. I couldn't remember her name. Fortunately, she wore a badge.

"I'm sorry, uh, Portia." I ducked my head, going through the motions of submissive body language I had learned about in Professor Luciano's lecture on shifters last week.

"So get back there already, pronto!" She took her hands off her hips and clapped them twice. I scuttled toward the swinging double doors, Grace following me.

"How can we spy from back here?" she whispered.

"We can't." I reached for a napkin, attempting to wrap it around a handful of silverware and failing miserably. "But that might be okay. Peek out the window."

Grace stood on her toes to peer through the round glass in one of the doors.

"Cadence is here?" Grace looked back over her shoulder, blinking at me.

"Yeah, I forgot she comes once a month for mimosas with her mom." I winced.

Grace snorted, padding quietly toward the bin of utensils and stacked napkins. She grabbed a fork, a knife, and a spoon, then raised an eyebrow. "So, we don't have to do any of this crazy crap?"

"You'd better do it five minutes ago." Portia breathed down our necks. "I've got a delivery to sign for. Get those done in that time, or you're out on your asses."

"Yes, ma'am." I reached for the tray of silverware, then nudged Grace with my elbow and jerked my chin at the stack of white linen napkins.

"Okay." She nodded.

We spent the next five minutes wrapping sets of forks knives and spoons in smooth, clean fabric. Neither of us knew what to do, let alone the Lyceum's particular style of silverware preparation, which was why we had to leave before the surly shifter returned.

But we didn't see a way out until Dylan walked by, following the manager. He glanced at us, jerking his thumb at the back entrance and waggling his eyebrows. Before he could elaborate, Dylan turned the corner as the manager explained to him how runners brought food from the refrigerator and stockroom to chefs in the kitchen.

"What should we do?"

"Slip out the back, I guess." I peeked around the corner, checking to see if the coast was clear. Once it was, I beckoned to Grace, and we tiptoed through the hall, scrunching down as we passed the kitchen in hopes no one would see us.

We stopped at the door, then ducked behind a stack of boxes as Portia glared at someone we couldn't see outside the service entrance. I did a few deep-breathing exercises, the kind I used to focus before running or playing Bishop's Row. Grace joined me, which meant this experience even had her rattled.

There's this assumption about umbral magi that somehow they're sneaky or love clandestine and mysterious activities, but my room-mate didn't fit that stereotype. She loved socializing, was extroverted, and had trouble keeping secrets unless it was a matter of life and death.

I reached out, hoping to steady her shaking. She nodded, looking in my eyes as we squeezed each other's hands. Finally, she seemed to relax. That was good because the words I heard almost made me freak out.

"You take what we got, or you'll be sleeping with fishes instead of signing for them." The voice was low but harsh like the speaker had been at a concert the night before, screaming their vocal cords raw.

"This seafood isn't up to the restaurant's standards." Portia cleared her throat. "Tell it to your boss."

"Our boss figured you'd say something like that. Remember where you came from, Portia. She'll put you back there if you're not careful, so you take what we got. Understand?"

"Yeah, I get it." I heard a low growl before Portia cut it off to continue, "You tell her this is the last time. I've been out since I graduated, Crow."

"Are you crazy?" I heard a metallic snick. "She's still my boss, and she's killed messengers before."

"You tell her or Crow is on my personal menu, silver switchblade be damned."

This Portia person sounds fun. I wish you could introduce us.

"Just shut up." I put my hand over my mouth immediately, but it was too late. Grace stared at me, eyes wider than saucers and nostrils flaring, on high alert.

"Who was that?" snarled Crow.

"A couple of incompetent bussers." I heard the scratchy sound of a pen on paper. "There, day-old fish accepted. Now get lost, preferably at the bottom of the sea."

"I'd say have a nice day, but that's not happening." The door slammed on the end of Crow's sentence, muffling his last word.

Grace and I hurried back to the relative safety of the silverware station. Portia found us there instead of hiding behind the boxes, but of course, we'd botched the entire napkin-folding assignment and found ourselves immediately and roughly escorted out the service entrance.

The moment the door closed behind us, I whipped out my phone and sent Cadence a text. Hopefully, she'd get it in time and manage to listen in on the scheming parental magi.

I started walking down the alley behind the Lyceum, heading toward Washington Street until Grace stopped me.

"We don't want to go out there looking like this," she said.

"Oh, yeah." I held hands with her and let her banish the Umbral magic holding up Azrael's glamour. Soon the magipsychic illusion dropped away from us, meaning we wouldn't be mistaken for anyone's buddy on the street.

"That was a bust." Grace shook her head. "We got nothing."

"I'm not sure about that." I looked up the side of the building next to us, then whistled for Ember. "A boss of something connected to restaurants, delivering illegal fish to ex-gang members seems like a pretty big deal."

"But it's not relevant. Our problem is this unholy alliance between dangerous families."

"Yeah, that's right, unless us overhearing that instead was a coincidence." I shrugged. "It's hard to tell about that stuff."

"I know." Grace nodded wearily. She perked up a bit when her moon hare Lune came hopping toward her, headbutting her ankle. "Has Professor Luciano taught you guys about coincidence tracking yet?"

"It's next on his syllabus." I sighed. "It would have been last week, but he wanted us to have some knowledge of shifters before the Gallows Hill's extramural contingent came to campus."

"Professor DeBeer stuck to critters that couldn't be familiars for some reason, so I'm in the same boat."

I yawned.

You need a nap.

"Or something else," I answered with my out-loud voice.

"Something else, what now?" Grace blinked.

"Something like a coffee from the Witch's Brew." I rubbed my eyes. "For whatever reason, I'm exhausted. Come on, my treat."

We headed around the corner on Washington Street, pacing toward Essex and our favorite place for coffee drinks.

As we sat with our espresso-based beverages, Cadence got back to me. Her text told us she'd sat on the other side of the restaurant from the shady magi and didn't hear anything they'd said. I showed the message to Grace.

"Back to the drawing board, I guess."

"Oh, well. You can't have everything."

"They have open mic night tomorrow." Grace jerked her thumb at the flier posted on the beam next to us. "Has Dylan been doing those?"

"He hasn't mentioned it. Why not ask him yourself?"

"Because he doesn't seem like he wants to talk yet." She took a sip of her drink. "I'm kind of waiting for him to come to me."

"I don't think that's a good idea, Grace." I shook my head. "He's really busted up, like he thinks you don't even want to be friends."

"Can you tell him that's not true?"

"I have." I sighed. "He's not buying it. It looks like you're leaving him behind from where I sit. Maybe you could apologize?"

"Oh." She held her cup, turning it but not drinking this time. It shook slightly.

"You don't want to be friends with Dylan?" I held my breath, waiting for her answer. A sense of disbelief fell over me, like a blanket fort collapsing.

"I'm saying that in the near future, he might not want to be friends with me." Grace stared at the remnants of foam in her cup.

"Can you fill me in on that?" My voice sounded like soda left out overnight. It must've been worse than even I thought because Ember curled more tightly around my shoulders, lifting her head to rub cheeks with me.

"I'm afraid *you* won't even want to be friends with me."

"Hey, even if something you do makes me angry, Grace, I'm still your friend. You know that, right?" I reached out, placing my hand palm up on the table between us.

"This is kind of a doozie. And a secret, too." She looked around the coffee shop.

I had a glance around too and recognized no one, not even from town. It seemed we'd decided to have our coffee during tourist hour.

"Go ahead, my lips are sealed." I looked her in the eye. "Even if it makes me angry, I promise."

Grace reached out across the table, taking my hand. She clasped it the entire time she told me her plans, including how she expected them to impact the new social dynamic with students from Messing and Gallows Hill on campus.

She was right. You're angry. Why not tell her instead of making a face like a constipated badger?

I kept my emotions to myself because her theories made sense, even if I'd never use her methods in a million years. Everything to do with dating and sex still baffled me.

Grace's entire demeanor changed after she told me her secret, which wouldn't be one for much longer anyway. At least she could be at peace for the rest of today, though I'd have to stay home. I couldn't trust my errant inside voice or my temper to keep quiet around people like Temperance Fairbanks and Alex Onassis. I said goodbye and told her I'd spend the night with my parents.

I stood outside the door to the Witch's Brew, watching her cross Essex Street and enter that day's door to Hawthorne Academy. Then I turned and stared through the window at the clock on the coffee shop's wall, waiting ten minutes.

After that, I hurried through the campus door, checked to see that Grace was in the cafeteria, and grabbed my knapsack with the personal care items I'd want overnight. After that, I went home to call my friends from town.

We met on the playground at our old elementary school.

"I'm sorry, Aliyah." Cadence kicked her feet, disturbing the layer of mulch under the swing she sat on. "If I'd known a half-hour earlier, I could've moved our seats."

"No, it was my fault. I should have remembered mother-daughter mock-mimosa Saturdays. I mean, you've brought us along to enough of them."

"If I never drink another champagne glass full of tonic water and orange juice, it'll be too soon." Izzy snorted. "No offense, but I'm hoping real mimosas are better than the kids' version."

"We'll wait quite a while to find out." Cadence sighed.

"Anyway, I figured today would be a good time for me to give you a heads-up about what you might have to deal with on my campus."

I filled my friends in on all the recent developments, except Grace's secret plan. They'd known of Alex's agreement last spring with Charity Fairbanks to terrorize vamps and other extrahumans, which helped them put all the new stuff in context.

"At least Grace is having some success countering Temperance with her brand of in-crowd. It's a good thing everybody likes Dorian, too." Cadence grinned.

"Everybody does *not* like Dorian." Izzy sucked her teeth. "He's a wild card, and that's the opposite of comforting to plenty of folks. Grace had to fake-date him. Otherwise, he might have been competition."

"Dylan would agree with you, Iz." I nodded. "He fills the margins of his notebooks with stuff like comfort the disturbed and disturb the comfortable. Dylan can barely stand being in the same room with him, and Logan is not himself around Dorian Spanos."

"That's because he likes him, duh." Cadence rolled her eyes. "I mean, come on. It's totally obvious."

"I thought I was the only one who noticed." I blinked. "And Grace, who's around Dorian all the time."

"I did too," Izzy said. "But I'm psychic, so take that with an entire can of salt."

"Did you tell Lee?" I raised an eyebrow.

"Why would I?"

I sat waiting for Cadence to say something, but she didn't.

"He took you to the Parents' Night dance, which is kind of a big deal to Hawthorn students."

"What's this?" Cadence stood up, the swing arcing back and forth behind her. She barely noticed as it smacked into her legs repeatedly.

"You went on a date? A real date, like wearing a dress and dancing, the whole nine yards?"

"It wasn't a date." Izzy waved her hand. "We're like partners in crime. Not romantic."

"I know you and Lee hang out alone in your house." Cadence tapped her foot, putting her hands on her hips. "So, what's going on?"

"That's between Lee and me." Izzy gazed steadily into Cadence's eyes. "It's none of your business."

"Okay." She reached behind her, grabbing for the swing, and sat back down. "Anyway, I think I can handle myself on your campus, Aliyah. It should be easy enough to avoid the mean crowd. And don't worry, I've already told everyone on our team who the cool kids are."

"What about you, Izzy?" I leaned an elbow on the picnic table, turning my head to look at my psychic friend.

"Yeah, the Messing folk should go your way for the most part. Jonah is the only one you have to worry about, not that I think the anti-vamp bigots will want anything to do with him."

"Oh, yeah, he's the psychic vampire." Cadence nodded. "What did he say about the ballroom dancing?"

"Yeah, we're teaming up for that. And we both made the Bishop's Row team, too." She sighed. "So your plan worked, Cadence."

"Who plays reverse point?" I wanted to know, so I could compare them to Elanor Pierce. I was prepared to do a little digging to figure out our chances of winning the tournament in the spring.

"Oh, that's me." Izzy looked down, tracing a smiley face carved into the surface of the picnic table.

I had nothing to say to that. Fortunately, any awkwardness Izzy might've noticed went unseen, thanks to Cadence's squeals of glee.

"Oh, my God, I can't believe it!" She clapped her hands. "Azrael's reverse point on our team. What position are you playing again, Aliyah?"

"Mid, with Dylan. Elanor Pierce is reverse point. She's badass, so watch out, Izzy."

"Good." Izzy finally looked up. "Maybe she'll strike Jonah out on the first throw."

"You still don't like the guy." Cadence shook her head. "What gives?"

"It's not that I don't like him." Izzy sighed. "He treats me like I'm his sister."

"Oh." I nodded, understanding. "You've had enough of that to last ten lifetimes."

"True story."

After that, we all stood up, then took a walk around the block. As we went, I filled them in on everything Grace and I had seen and heard in the kitchen. Cadence kept her mouth shut the whole time, which I thought was odd. When we got to Hawthorn Street, I was about to check on her, but Dylan Khan ran up to us and interrupted.

"Aliyah, thanks!" His grin was wider than I'd seen it since before Grace broke up with him outside the Engine House.

"What? Why?" I blinked.

"The Lyceum hired me. Even if the café stays closed all year, I'll make enough money to afford tuition again."

"I've been meaning to ask, Dylan." Cadence tilted her head. "You have to work two jobs just to come to school. Why aren't you on a scholarship?"

The grin faded, and the spark in his eyes dulled.

"Cadence." Izzy elbowed her. "Apologize, jeez."

"No, it's okay." Dylan shook his head. "Because I don't qualify for the need-based ones. My folks don't make a lot of money, but it's too much for financial aid. I got something the first year from a poetry contest, but that was a one-shot deal, and I'll never make grades like Logan."

"Oh." Cadence shook her head. "That's too bad."

"Hey," I tugged Dylan's sleeve, "you just got a job. We should celebrate. I'll get us some pizza, then we can play *Mario Kart* at my place."

"That sounds awesome." His smile returned, not as big as last time, but still, it was a comfort. Like watching Ember flying toward me.

I took up my phone and called the pizza place, making our order for pickup. We got the order and walked back to my house, joking and laughing like we had the summer before freshman year. The next day, all four of us would be in the same school at the same time, though it wasn't easy to forget we'd still be separated into teams. It wouldn't be as simple as before.

You can't deliberately take yourself or your friends back in time to when life was simpler, but sometimes, when you're together, it happens on its own.

CHAPTER EIGHT

After breakfast on Sunday, all the Hawthorn students lined the walkway leading from the foyer door to the seating in front of the podium. We waited, watching as students from the Messing and Gallows Hill schools filed past.

The Messing kids kept to themselves, walking with their heads either down or turned toward each other. They didn't fall into a single-file line, but their red-accented gray uniforms gave that impression.

The one exception was Izzy, who kept her head up and locked gazes with everyone she knew from Hawthorn. A freckled redheaded boy walked near her, staring straight ahead. His hazel eyes seemed to look at everything and nothing at the same time, a Mona Lisa smile giving the impression that he knew more than he should about our school. The rest of the psychics reminded me of autumn rain pattering against a bedroom window—uniform, gray, and relentless.

The Gallows Hill students came through the door behind them, their attitude and behavior a night-and-day difference. They were raucous, loud, and vital, like confetti and bullhorns, with one exception.

Brianna Collins brought up the rear, her hands clasped in front of her so tightly her knuckles looked like sun-bleached driftwood. I gave her my best smile, hoping to ease the anxiety I knew she always felt in large crowds. She didn't return the smile but she straightened, walking with more confidence after that.

Cadence glanced over her shoulder, blinking at me and tilting her head in Brianna's direction. I wasn't sure what that meant but figured the mermaid would tell me later.

As instructed, all the Hawthorn students waited for the others to take their assigned seats before choosing our own. It was the first time I ended up closer to the rear for a formal announcement here. I didn't much like it because it wasn't easy to focus on the headmaster's speech. Fortunately, most of it was stuff I already knew about campus.

Headmaster Hawkins tapped the lectern and the magipsychic screen lit up, displaying a map of campus. He pointed out the locations of the cafeteria, the academic wing, including classrooms reopened for guests to use and the infirmary, then moved on to announce that the Gallows Hill students had accommodations on the fourth floor, with Messing's on the fifth.

He introduced the professors and coaches on our faculty, then moved on to the visiting staff from the other schools. Each contingent had an administrator, an academic instructor, an athletic coach, and an artistic mentor. Messing also brought a nurse. When he introduced the administrator from Gallows Hill, his voice cracked.

"It's my mom." Hal murmured from behind me.

"Are you okay?" I didn't dare turn around in my seat but had to ask.

"Yeah. She's here practically by herself, and I've got all my friends with me."

"If she messes with you, give the word, and she's TKO." Faith's voice carried genuine menace, and I could hardly blame her.

After that, we quieted down because Headmaster Hawkins changed the magipsychic display to show us a list of all the extramural competitions running until late next spring.

"Most of you have seen this before. The first of these is Magipsychic Fair, and we've got some special guests to run that for you on campus and in town over the next three weekends." Headmaster Hawkins stepped aside from the podium, then extended his hand.

Two figures emerged from the hallway beside the stairs. I blinked, nearly standing up in my surprise because I recognized them both from the Providence news bulletins the last few years.

"May I introduce Mr. Blaine Harcourt and Miss Kim Ichiro. He's a doctoral candidate at Providence Paranormal College, and she works for the Newport Police Department. You might have noticed the magipsych projects have themes in their areas of expertise. That's because they'll be judging them." He grinned, then glanced at Kim. "You had a few words, Miss Ichiro?"

"Thanks, Headmaster." The young woman grinned, nodding her head. Her nut-brown ponytail bobbed, showing off the nearly blonde hair at the tips. "We're very excited to help with the kickoff event for your extramurals. Your headmaster was right about one thing: it'll be challenging, but you will definitely have a blast. I can't wait to see what you make together!"

It was hard not to look at the Tanuki as she spoke. Her manner was engaging and her voice carried an undercurrent of fun and excitement, but I couldn't help glancing at Blaine Harcourt. He didn't look happy to be here, not one bit. When I noticed his eyes fixed on a spot somewhere behind me, I realized what his problem was.

"Hal, he's scared of Nin."

"But she's harmless."

"Pharaoh's rats are the only natural predators dragon shifters have."

"Crap. How could I forget something like that?"

"Shush." Bailey elbowed me. "They're still talking."

"Sorry."

She was right, but all we had missed was the headmaster dismissing us to mingle in the lobby and that the magipsychic display would introduce each student guest momentarily.

It wasn't easy to pay attention to the displays. I was too busy being pulled around the room between Grace, Izzy, and Cadence, and in all that mess, I had to check on Hal and Dylan. Dorian kept Logan near him most of the time, ushering him into a huddle with Grace, Kitty, and Eston.

I was surprised when a cold hand closed around my wrist. I twisted out of its grasp, turning abruptly and narrowing my eyes at the pale red-haired boy from Messing Academy. His eyes were wide and round, his mouth open like a fish out of water's.

"Who do you think you are?" I put my hands on my hips.

"Peep!" Ember reared up on my shoulder, her wings stretched wide and her breath hot against my cheek.

"Um, Jonah Arnold." He blinked, then composed his expression, but I could tell it was a façade. I'd frightened him. "I know your Izzy. I mean, your friend." He cleared his throat. "Your friend Izzy. We're ballroom dancing partners, and she talks about you all the time."

"So, you thought you could just grab me?" I tapped my foot. "If she talks about me, you know I'm a fire magus, right?"

"Extramagus, actually." He gave me a full smile, including a set of pointy fangs not long enough to signal bloodthirst. "And I'm a vampire, so I guess we are both slightly more dangerous than our peers in a manner of speaking."

"I'd rethink that if I were you." I rubbed my wrist. His grip had been stronger than anything I was used to. "I'm only dangerous to my enemies. Don't make yourself one of them."

"Look, I'm sorry." The smile vanished, replaced by a thin straight line. "I assumed you knew as much about me as I did about you. That we'd meet as friends."

"You didn't pay much attention to what Izzy leaves unspoken, then, and nobody I know is cool with randomly handsy guys."

"I screwed up. I'll apologize more profusely if that helps. It's just, I thought maybe we could talk Bishop's Row. We're both playing on our school teams, after all."

"Maybe later. I've got a lot to do right now." I shook my head, trying to settle my nerves. Jonah had scared me, too. His forwardness reminded me too much of Alex Onassis. "And maybe you're right. I'm slightly dangerous, but mostly harmless."

"I don't buy that for a second." He sighed. "It sounds too much like the kind of thing I'd say about myself. Anyway, for the third time, I make my apologies and invite you to approach me next time. I'll leave you alone unless you do, I promise."

I rolled my eyes and walked away because I wasn't sure how to respond to that. Also, I'd noticed Dylan edging toward the corner again, isolating himself. He shouldn't have to do that, considering Cadence and Izzy were here and nowhere near Grace.

"I just need a minute, Aliyah." He held up a hand, palm out.

"Okay." I glanced over my shoulder. "But Cadence is making a beeline over here. Should I stop her?"

"Head her off for a second if you don't mind." Dylan closed his eyes. "I just need to take a couple of breaths."

"Hey, Cadence." I stepped in front of my friend.

"Hey, yourself." She grinned. "I just wanted to introduce Dylan to a couple of the guys on our Bishop's Row team. Oh, and Brianna wants to see you."

"Okay." I nodded. "He'll be along in a minute. Where's Brianna?" I looked around, not seeing her immediately.

"Trying to find the restroom. For whatever reason, she's gotten super-shy all of a sudden."

"Oh." I blinked. I couldn't imagine Brianna Collins, the queen of customer service, being shy. Her trouble with crowds had more to do with ambient noise than people.

"Yeah, I don't get it either." She shrugged. "Anyway, she must have found the restroom because I don't see her anymore."

"Hello, Cadence." Dylan stepped up beside me. "How're things?"

"I could ask you the same."

" I wouldn't answer right now. Maybe later." He jerked his chin at a crowd of Gallows Hill students. "I couldn't help but overhear you want me to meet some people. Shall we?"

"Okay." Cadence jerked her thumb in the direction of the restrooms. "Maybe you want to go in after her, Aliyah?"

"Will do."

Somehow yet another friend needed my help at this gathering. At least Dylan was in good hands. I glanced back over my shoulder at Hal and Faith, entrenched by the door to the lounge, chatting with Darren. They seemed safe enough, but Alex and Temperance stood by the now-empty podium, glaring daggers at Jonah. I couldn't make myself scarce in the ladies' room while a vampire sat alone in a corner with those two around. Fortunately, the perfect person happened to walk right past me. I stopped her with a smile.

"Hey, Elanor, there's someone you should meet."

"Really?" She blinked, then shook her head. "Of course. You have friends all over town, so you know some of these students."

I beckoned her to follow me, then sauntered toward Jonah and made introductions. He knew something about performance art in case they ran out of Bishop's Row topics. I'd done what I could for him. It seemed like the right call, too, since Temperance turned her back and stalked away, Alex in tow.

In the bathroom, Brianna was nowhere to be seen, but one of the stalls was closed, so I figured she was in there. I checked my makeup in the mirror, which wasn't necessary, considering I'd only put on a little lip gloss. After that, just for something to do, I washed my hands. The noise must've alerted her to my presence because a moment later, Brianna emerged from the stall.

Her face was blotchy, her color too high. I saw that in the mirror as she leaned forward to wash her hands, even though she hadn't flushed. So she hadn't been in the stall for its intended purpose. She'd been crying.

"Are you okay?"

"I wish I could say yes." She shrugged.

"Do you want to talk about it?" I leaned against the counter. "I'm here if you do. And our headmaster is also a licensed counselor if you need that."

"It's just, in order to do these extramurals, I had to quit at Walgreens, and I don't know what I'm going to do after that."

"Oh, Brianna. That sucks. Why?"

"I'll be missing most of the holiday season in retail, that's why."

"Dylan didn't say anything about that."

"He quit when he got the Lyceum job. Anyway, we're confined to campus except for school breaks and weekends. That's not enough hours for retail in autumn."

"I had no idea they were doing that."

"Me either, not until after I signed up."

"And you couldn't drop? Or ask for an exception?"

"I tried. Principal Hawkins said no."

"Do you want me to talk to my mom? She might be able to help since she works in extrahuman education."

"It's too late for that. My job's already gone, and next year I'll probably be back in Billerica at the public school."

"Let's not count on that. This is Salem, so there are loads of places you can work."

"I'll have maybe a week and a half after extramurals end."

"Well, you'll have help, don't worry."

"Thanks. You don't know how much that means."

"I'm trying to start a kindness trend. People should help each other."

She blinked, standing perfectly still. She opened her mouth but closed it again, whatever she was going to say lost in the silence between us. After that, Brianna reached for a paper towel, wet it, and wiped her face. Moments later, she strode out the door, shoulders back and head held high.

"I guess our work here is done, girl."

Ember peeped happily from her perch on my shoulder, and we headed out of the bathroom. By that time, the presentation was over and I'd missed my chance to put all the faces together with the names of the visiting students.

I watched as Elanor introduced Jonah to Noah. The two of them acted like bosom buddies. Hopefully, I'd made the right call. I headed toward where Cadence stood with Dylan, Logan, and a couple of familiar characters. I'd seen them before and meant to reintroduce myself but never made it over there.

Grace unleashed her secret plan.

It wasn't as devastating as the scene outside the Engine House, but just as unmistakable to everyone in the room. Dorian Spanos was getting dumped by Grace Dubois. She shook her finger at him, eyes narrowed and color high. He leaned back slightly, arms crossed over his chest, staring down his nose. Mercy perched on his shoulder, cawing at Lune, who turned his back on the gryphon and leaned against Grace's calf.

She rolled her eyes one final time. He shrugged in response. When they parted, the room went silent for almost five seconds. After that, a cacophony of whispers, speculation, and rumor filled the air. Finally, a bell chimed, signaling that the guests' rooms were ready.

I yawned as the visiting students got their room assignments at the pneumatic tubes. I supposed that one upside to the drastically reduced enrollment at Hawthorn was that we had the space for an event like this.

When Grace came to collect me and head back to our room, I was so exhausted I took a nap, something that hadn't happened in years. I didn't wake up until it was time for lunch.

CHAPTER NINE

At lunch, the cafeteria wasn't filled to capacity, even with all the visiting students. The Gallows Hill corner was loud and tight-knit. I wondered what it would've been like if we'd visited their campus instead of the other way around. I laughed, trying to imagine it, which wasn't easy because I'd only ever seen pictures of their athletic facilities.

"Aliyah, hi." Azrael Ambersmith stepped up behind me in the food line. "Can I sit with you guys?"

"Let me guess, you need a break from that noisy crew?" I raised my eyebrow at his classmates, who had pushed several rectangular tables together to make one enormous seating arrangement.

"Bingo!" he exclaimed. "I'm from a big family, but my classmates take the cake. I'm glad you understand. But mostly, I wanted to ask something if it was okay."

"Why wouldn't it be okay? You're my friend."

"There's a little more to it than that."

He glanced toward the row of booths, including the one Hal had staked out for us at the beginning of last year. The kids from our year had taken them over, turning around to chat with each other. The one exception was Grace, who paced in front of them, stopping at each booth to socialize with everybody.

"Wait a minute." I put my hand on his shoulder. "Wait just a minute there, Az. Are you trying to tell me—"

"That I want to ask Grace on a date?"

"Well, no, I thought it was maybe a little bigger and more long term than that."

"She doesn't seem to be very long-term right now." He shook his head. "But do you think she'd say yes?"

"Well, she just broke up with Dorian." I jerked my chin at everyone's favorite goth kid. "But they were only platonic, really."

"Yeah, I saw." Azrael composed his face, speaking flatly. "And plenty of people have deep connections without romance. There's no "only" about it, you know?"

"I don't." I sighed. "I'm probably the worst person to talk to about relationship stuff. Have you tried Cadence?"

"You're Grace's roommate and one of her closest friends, so I figured you're the best person to ask."

"Az, she's not following her heart right now. I don't want either of you to get hurt."

"I know. This last month and the whole situation with Dylan was hard on her."

"Nowhere near as hard as it was for him, though." I blinked.

"No, you're wrong." He shook his head. "I worked with her all summer, so I saw it. She was busted up weeks before they split. It wasn't easy for her."

"She's run everything strategically since then, like a computer." I sighed. "I mean, she talked a little with me, but like it happened last year instead of last month."

"That's Grace, for you." He shrugged. "Keeps anything thorny at arm's length. Anyway, if you think she'll listen, I'll go ask."

"Right now?" I blinked. She'd planned the breakup with Dorian but had said nothing about Azrael. "Are you sure?"

"There's no time like the present." He grinned. "Thanks, Aliyah."

Before I could say anything else, he stepped out of the line and headed toward Grace. I stood there, staring so intently I forgot where I was for a moment.

"It's your turn, already." I glanced over my shoulder to find my brother, rolling his eyes at me.

"Sorry, Noah." I stepped up to the window and made my order, then moved over to wait and let him make his.

"I'll have what she's having," he told the cook.

"So, how are you doing?"

"Not that it's any of your business, but not bad." Noah studied his nails.

"Not bad is pretty good, right?"

"It isn't, but it doesn't totally suck either."

I laughed. I couldn't help it because Noah was just so contrary and perfectly himself right at that moment. Even though I missed how close we used to be, having this exchange with him, however brief, felt precious somehow.

He didn't laugh with me or even at me. I'm not sure he could have mustered anything as free and open as true laughter just then. Noah's biggest flaw might be holding grudges for too long, but the runner-up was taking himself too seriously. I knew that feeling all too well, which was why I felt a momentary surge of euphoria when he smiled.

"Maybe things will be pretty good, you know, eventually." My order came up, so I reached out to move my plate from the counter to my tray.

"Some stuff needs work, but yeah." He nodded, getting his own sandwich from the counter. "I think you're right for once."

He walked away before I did, not even stopping to get a beverage before heading to the biggest round table, where he sat beside Elanor. Jonah immediately defected from the cluster of Messing folk in the far corner to sit on his other side.

"Don't get too comfortable, Morgenstern." Alex tried his best to look down his nose at me.

"You have no say in how I feel about anything."

"This is a warning. Your brother had better watch who he spends time with."

"Your threats suck. I already said I'm not afraid of you."

"A warning, Aliyah." Alex stared into my eyes, unblinking. His were bloodshot and blotchy like Brianna's. "About something. It's not a threat from *me*, and you'd do well to remember that."

He stepped across the way, stopping in front of the DIY sandwich station. He didn't even have a tray, just stuffed some bread and a handful of peanut butter containers into a paper bag and made a beeline out of the cafeteria.

"What was that about, I wonder?" Dorian held a pair of empty tumblers, waggling them at me. "Never mind. Beverage roulette?"

"Sure." I reached out, taking one of the cups and joining him at the soda dispenser.

"Ooh, it's good this time." He grinned at his improvised drink.

I took a sip of my own, then wrinkled my nose. "Too much orange soda."

"You can't win them all." He shrugged, then led the way toward our friends.

We sat with Logan, who'd been by himself at a booth. Hailey joined us, peering at our drinks before inquiring about what they were. Dorian explained beverage roulette, then got up to help her make her own. He seemed unperturbed that Azrael and Grace stood in the corner together, clearly flirting.

"Is he going to be to be okay with that?" Bailey asked from the booth behind us. "Dorian, I mean."

"Doesn't seem to bother him." Logan shrugged, bowing his head, but I noticed his face turning red.

"Goths, am I right?" Bailey snorted, then went back to her food.

I didn't see how the incident started because my back was turned. I'd thought everything was fine, too. So much for all my practice at empathy.

A piercing shriek, the kind that makes rodents in an open field cringe with terror, almost dropped me to the floor. It was so loud and shrill it felt like an ice pick through my inner ear. The edges of my vision wobbled a bit.

Despite the dizziness, I turned and looked around. All I saw was a blur of white and blue circling the two boys in the middle of the dining room.

Dylan's fists were twisted in the lapels of Dorian's blazer. The fabric looked stiff like it had been in the freezer for a week. I couldn't see Dylan's face, but Dorian's face was a rictus of terror.

You can see his breath. Dangerous. Did your ersatz boyfriend ever talk to his professor about being an extramagus, I wonder?

"I said, sorry!"

"Not good enough, Spanos." Dylan growled. Like, actually growled, sounding like a wolf in winter, desperate for prey.

"What are you?" Dorian's eyes bulged, more of the cornea visible than usual. They rolled as he looked around for some way, any way, out of Dylan's grasp.

"Your worst nightmare."

Before their exchange progressed, their familiars plunged down from somewhere near the ceiling. Mercy and Gale were a tangle of wings. Gale's tail lashed through the air, striking the furred part of Mercy's back. I saw why the next moment. Mercy's beak had scratched the scales under Gale's eye, leaving a bloody red welt.

"Peep!"

Ember leaped off my shoulder and rose high, hiding behind the light from the chandelier. I couldn't see her but felt the change in her gravity as she swooped toward the fighting pair.

Just in time, she grabbed them with her talons, pulling up to slow their fall as much as she could. It could've been worse since gryphons are fragile, and breaking a dragonet's fall could severely injure them. Despite Ember making sure Mercy wasn't crushed, their landing was still catastrophic.

"Ow!" Kitty jumped up, cranberry juice splashing all over the front of her blouse. She held one hand to her mouth as the other one dropped the fork she'd been holding.

"Paralysis!"

D.R. PERRY

The voice came from the doorway where Professor DeBeer stood, feet planted. Her lightning bird perched on her shoulders with his wings outstretched. I could see a crackle of energy arcing from his beak to the polished length of wood in her hand.

Wandwork and familiar magic. She must have several advanced degrees.

The effect was immediate, Gale, Mercy, and Ember sprawled across the table, frozen in place, the three of them lying still in the now-ruined victuals. But the Professor hadn't gotten anywhere near the root of the problem.

"He started it." Dorian's eyes went wide, breath pluming like smoke in the space between them.

"You started it when you stole my girlfriend." Dylan's hair seemed to go white in places, while Dorian's blew back from his face.

"You split before I got here."

"Boys, no fighting." Professor Luciano paced from the food line toward my friends, hands outstretched. "You should know better, Mr. Spanos. You're on probation, after all. And Mr. Khan. You've worked so hard to be here. Don't squander it on fighting."

A moment later, he placed his hand on Dylan's shoulder. Luciano's eyes went wide. He stared as though seeing him for the first time, then sighed, eyes going limpid with empathy.

"Enough." Professor DeBeer paced toward Luciano. After that, I couldn't believe my ears or my eyes. "My student, my problem."

She pushed him. Not some elementary schoolyard shove, either. Her hand channeled enough lightning to make me see spots.

Professor Luciano flew across the room, his back crashing against the table where Hal and Faith sat. He struggled to rise but winced and held his back with one hand.

"Professor!" Hal grabbed Luciano's free hand but looked at Faith. "Get Dad."

She sprang to action, leaping off the booth's bench and fleeing the cafeteria.

"You lying, scheming freak!" Professor DeBeer's eyes narrowed, her hands crackling with lightning as she homed in on Dylan. I never

82

imagined she'd ever look this feral or threatening, especially not toward a student. Her temper was higher than Dylan's the moment before, and lightning was one of the most dangerous magics out there.

But I couldn't figure out why Dylan's teacher reacted with alarm. Hadn't he gone to her about his extramagus status the first week of school?

It doesn't matter now. You've got more power than anyone else in this room, even her. Use it unless you want this to get worse.

"No." I broke into a flat sprint, reaching my friends before Professor DeBeer. I stepped into the middle of the cluster, skin humping up into gooseflesh. It felt like the middle of February in a lightning storm, but I wanted to do this mundanely unless my hand got forced somehow.

"Get out of my way, Morgenstern," Professor DeBeer snarled.

"I want to help."

"That's what your kind always say." She turned, stretching one electrified hand toward me. "At least at the beginning. One of you on campus was enough. Two are untenable. See what happens when you lose control? Everyone's in danger, and it's your fault."

Every impulse in my body urged me to step back and drag the boys with me, away from the high-voltage magus, but I held my ground, shaking my head.

"We're kids." I couldn't look into her eyes, afraid I'd find something in them as terrifying to me as a slayer was to a vampire. "We make mistakes. Get in fights."

"Like the one last year when you nearly burned this room down? I've had enough of extramagi and their ruination to last a lifetime." Her eyes went wide, something in them broken. Her gaze turned inward, maybe at some future fear or past horror. "You should have been expelled ages ago."

I had nothing to say to that. Even the Evil Inside Voice stayed silent. I swallowed, unable to get past the lump in my throat, even if I'd had words at the ready.

It's easy to think of something after the fact, a zinger or defiant statement on your right to exist. But when I stood face to face with someone who considered me less than human, my ability to act narrowed. My options got honed down to a single point. I was lucky to just stay put.

So I stood and trembled. My entire body felt wavery, like heat rising off blacktop in the middle of summer. But it was cold, and finally, I had an idea. Simple, maybe too easy, but it'd have to do. I couldn't talk Professor DeBeer down, but she wasn't the only participant in this conflict.

"Dylan, let it go."

Professor Luciano and Hal leaned on each other, looking as unsteady as I felt. Kitty rushed to their rescue, inserting herself between them and getting her shoulders under their arms. The cranberry stain on her silvery gray blouse stood out like a wound.

"He has everything, Aliyah." Dylan's voice stretched almost pleadingly, like he wanted my permission to hurt our classmate. "And he hasn't worked a day in his life for any of it."

"Understood, Mr. Khan." Professor Luciano took a deep breath. "But this situation has more wires than a pipe bomb, and the only way to defuse it is if someone steps down."

"Ask your colleague." Dylan's gaze moved from Dorian to DeBeer. "I thought she was in my corner."

"Isn't that what they hired us to do?" Professor Luciano tilted his head, raising his eyebrow. "Support our students?"

"*He* is the bomb, Lucy." Professor DeBeer shook her head. "Not the situation. Look at him—both ice and air, and bound to do evil and harm."

Dylan's jaw dropped, his face paling as much as it could for someone with his complexion, and his eyes widened. The professor's words hit like a slap, and I knew too well how it felt when someone you trusted weaponized their words.

A moment later, his eyes narrowed. I watched him, wondering because it didn't look like anything I'd felt. Then I remembered the Evil Inside Voice and how it encouraged me to follow impulses. Did Dylan have one in his head?

"You want evil?" Dylan took a deep breath. The air around him got so cold my eyebrows frosted over. "You want harm?"

Across the room, Izzy raised her hand. She held a card up, the Devil reversed. It meant I had to step up and try to take Dylan with me.

"No." I countered. "You're better than this." I stood up straight. "Stand down with me."

"I'm sick of it. Turn the other cheek, be the better man. With grades, with money, and now magic." He turned his head, arctic gaze meeting mine. "But I'll do it for you, Aliyah."

Just like that, the cold vanished. Dylan untangled his hand from Dorian's jacket. Professor DeBeer shut off her lightning, releasing the familiars from their paralysis at the same time. They scuttled across the table. Mercy came up covered in the remains of Kitty's soup, a crouton hanging from her beak.

"Mr. Khan. My office. Now." Headmaster Hawkins' voice boomed through the cafeteria.

"Sir, can I—"

"No, Miss Morgenstern. I'll talk to witnesses later."

"What about my colleague?" Professor Luciano rubbed his back, glaring at Professor DeBeer.

"As I said, later." Headmaster Hawkins looked at Dylan. "I'll listen to Mr. Khan's account of events before doing anything else."

Dylan followed the headmaster, glancing back over his shoulder before exiting the cafeteria. He looked shell-shocked, like he couldn't believe what had just happened.

In the far corner, Temperance Fairbanks held her grundylow and smiled. Alex leaned against the wall near her, gazing at the floor.

"Well, Izzy." I turned to look at my psychic friend, "you wanted to see how magi go to school, right?"

"Not like this." She shook her head, holding up her hand to reveal another card.

It was the Tower reversed, just about the worst card anyone with catastrophic levels of power could get. Dylan Khan, as it turned out, had that in spades.

CHAPTER TEN

"Thanks." Dorian caught up with me at the stairs, Mercy cradled in his arms. "For what you did back there, talking Dylan down."

"I didn't do it for you." Ember lifted her head, peering out at him from under my hair, then shot me a withering look. "Sorry. That was mean."

"Help was help, whoever you meant it for." He patted Mercy, sighing over all the condiments and other cafeteria detritus in her feathers and fur. "And this dirty birdie needs a little help from Irish Spring."

"Do you ever take anything seriously?" I stepped onto the moving staircase, and he followed. Izzy caught up, standing a few steps down. "That was a bad scene, Dorian."

"Everybody saw Grace's breakup theater." He leaned against the railing. "And some other guy just asked her out. I couldn't have predicted Dylan would go extramagus on my hiney. And why shouldn't I crack jokes?"

"Was I a goofball back there?" I raised an eyebrow.

"Well, no." He sighed. "But serious isn't my style."

"Bury the hatchet with him. We can't be at each other's throats all year, with Temperance just waiting for us to mess up."

"You have a point, but I can't do it."

"You might have to," Izzy said. "Cards don't lie."

We rode it in silence. At our stop, Izzy ushered us along the third-floor hall.

"So, I have to make nice with Dylan?" Dorian tilted his head at her. "He's the one in trouble."

"I pulled that Tower card for Dylan, but you were the focus of his anger when I did it."

"Would you mind giving me a full reading?" He wrinkled his nose, waving a hand at Mercy. "After she gets cleaned up."

"What?" She blinked.

"Is that so strange?" He asked. "A gryphon having a bath?"

"No, the reading. Usually, magi don't want them."

"My parents are psychics." He shrugged. "For me, it's comforting."

"Well, in that case, sure. My room's on the fifth floor."

"We can use mine." I jerked my thumb down the hall. "Grace is in Creatives, working on a project. I can even give Mercy a bath while you do it." Each room at Hawthorn had a fully stocked grooming station accessible through a panel in the wall.

"Okay, then." Dorian nodded. "Let's go."

I let them into my room, clearing off my desk so Izzy had a surface to work on. After that, I opened the grooming panel, ran water, and added soap. Mercy flew over, ducking and splashing in it like a giant birdbath. At least she liked getting clean.

Anything could happen in Izzy's reading. She'd been precognitive from an early age and had lots of practice, but her abilities had no obligation to follow our social agenda. I hoped Izzy could convince him to make an effort with Dylan.

You can't save all of your friends from his anger. The Ambersmith boy might be his next enemy.

"At least he's not in our class." I put my hand over my mouth, getting suds on my chin.

"I don't know. The headmaster might make him switch with someone." Dorian took my statement in his own context. "Considering what DeBeer said about extramagi back there."

"Oh." I blinked. I hadn't mentioned my inside voice to him, so naturally, he'd thought I'd said something sensible.

"It looks like Dorian's got something." Izzy tapped the card she'd just flipped, the Two of Wands reversed. "He'll have to work with someone he doesn't like in the very near future."

"That could mean a number of people, actually." Dorian sighed. "I'm not sure why Grace installed me in the in-crowd. I'm the least popular third-year guy."

"You have your fans." Izzy tapped another card, the Five of Cups. "Somebody here thinks you're awesome, all shiny and sparkly."

I held my tongue, not mentioning Logan. It was up to him and Dorian to figure that out, and maybe the reading wasn't about romance anyway. Last year, I'd had more friends than expected. Why not Dorian?

"What I really want to know is, will I get expelled?"

"Okay." She nodded, flipping over the four of swords. "That's unlikely. That problem's in the past."

"So, all I have to do is stay out of trouble?" He rolled his eyes. "Not as easy as it looks."

"You've got a student mentor, remember?" I grinned. "Logan's looking out for you."

"Ha." Izzy flipped another card. "Yeah, it looks like you need more support. Logan's a water magus, right, Aliyah?"

"That he is." I nodded. "Why?"

"Check it out." She held up the card. It was the Page of Cups.

"I forget what that one means." I gave Mercy's back a good scrubbing.

"I know it." Dorian sighed. "My sister worked with cards some-times too."

Neither of them divulged the card's meaning, just exchanged glances that didn't include me. I kept my thoughts to myself, hoping it was positive.

"But that's not enough." Izzy shook her head.

"Okay, okay." Dorian sighed. "Aliyah's right. I have to talk to Dylan."

"Bring a friend." She tapped the next card, the Knight of Swords.

"Dylan used to have a long fuse, but not right now. I had no idea he was an extramagus, either."

I busied myself with changing the soapy water out for fresh. Mercy ducked under the faucet's stream, shaking her feathery little head in the flowing water. Ember peeped from my shoulder, then splashed down to join her.

"Aliyah didn't seem surprised," Dorian said.

"He told me last month. Said he'd talk to Professor DeBeer about it." I close my eyes. "I watched him request a meeting with her that same day, too."

"But tonight, she was the opposite of helpful." Izzy sighed. "Sounds like she's got a hate on for extramagi."

I shook my head. "Enough about that. You're still doing Dorian's reading."

"Almost done." She flipped the last card. "Well, this is frigging great."

Dorian leaned back, his face paling. "The Devil never is unless you're about to go to a party."

"Even then, your fun's gonna be laced with trouble." Izzy shook her head. "This year's a minefield, so we'll have to watch out for each other. Which includes Dylan."

"She's all clean." I wrapped a towel around Mercy, patted her dry, and helped her back to Dorian's shoulder. When I turned, Ember had perched on the edge of the bath, waiting for her own towel and rubbing a patchy spot on her tail. I got her dry and applied some oil.

Izzy cleared her cards away, then helped me put the chairs back. We left the room, heading out to mingle with the other students.

"You want me to what?"

I didn't recognize the voice coming from the newly reopened café, so I peeked around the corner and found Kim Ichiro cornered by her fiancé. She saw me, so I nonchalantly headed to the counter. The manager stood behind it, waiting for someone in the throng of people staring at the menu to order something already.

"I'll have my usual, thanks."

"Caramel latte with soymilk coming up." She busied herself making my drink, giving me the perfect opportunity to listen in on the conversation behind me.

"Bring Cosmo to campus." Blaine Harcourt's voice was at low volume, but nasal and tinny enough for me to hear it.

"Why?"

"Have you seen the boy catch mice? I'll be safer from those homicidal rodents the Hawkins family carries around if he's here."

"Wait a minute." She cleared her throat. "You want a thirteen-year-old boy around all these upperclassmen? In cat form, no less?"

"Exactly." I caught Blaine's nod out of the corner of my eye. "I'm his godfather, and we can protect each other."

"Put on your big dragon pants, Blaine." She poked his chest with her index finger. "Familiars are bonded to their magi. Besides, Hal's a sweetie, and Nin's kind of cute."

"What if an unbonded one comes along?"

"The Headmaster says the only Pharaoh's rats on campus are his and his son's. They're both female, too, so they can't breed."

"I'm not entirely sure I believe that."

The cafe manager handed me my drink. I was about to let them have their conversation and not interfere, but Blaine's face was pale and sweaty, and his hands shook so much that tea sloshed over the rim of his cup. A nervous dragon shifter might vindicate folks who considered shifters too dangerous for campus.

"Excuse me, I couldn't help but overhear. Maybe I can reassure you."

"And you are?" Blaine raised his eyebrow. He also took a step back, allowing Kim to escape the corner and approach.

"She's the Morgenstern girl." She tilted her head, blinking. "Fred Redford said she helped put the fire out at the Night Creatures concert last Halloween."

He shook his head. "I don't see how a student can help in this situation."

"Let her talk, Blaine." I thought Kim might elbow him in the ribs, but she linked her arm through his instead. "Listening can't hurt."

"Okay."

"My grandmother's the extraveterinarian who licenses the familiars here. She keeps a public record of every critter on campus at her office down the street."

"I'm more worried about the off-record ones." Blaine wrinkled his nose. "They could be hiding in secret passages or something."

"There's a book about Hawthorn Academy in the library." I shrugged. "It's got blueprints, maps, and information about all the magical systems in here. It's reassuring."

"Wait a minute." He raised his eyebrow. "Are you a brainiac?"

"No, that's my friend Logan. He had his own concerns about campus security and felt way better after reading it. Maybe it could help you too."

"Come on, Blaine, you love libraries, and we haven't seen the one here yet." Kim did elbow him this time, but gently.

"I suppose it can't hurt. Lead on, Morgenstern."

I brought them to the academic wing, where they both paused at the stained glass windows in the doors. Kim pulled out her phone, asked me to stop, and took pictures before I led them through.

Once we got to the library, I introduced them to the Ashfords, who were busy stamping books. After that, Blaine marched directly toward the index in the middle and flipped through it.

"Wow." He shook his head. "Mr. Waban would have a field day in here."

"Is he the librarian from your old high school?"

"Hardly." Blaine sniffed. "He's the oldest dragon in North America, though he did fill in as librarian at Providence Paranormal for a couple of years."

"I thought your mother was the oldest dragon here?"

"Mr. Waban has at least two centuries on her." He tapped the page under his finger. "Is this it? *Hawthorn Academy: a Study in Between-World Architecture.*"

I nodded. "Yes."

"Smashing." He headed through the stacks, leaving Kim standing beside the index with me.

"I thought he was scared. What happened?" I asked.

"Blaine's a fire dragon, but this is his real element." Her smile carried loads of pride. "If you put him in a library, the rest of the world goes away. Thanks for bringing us here."

"You're guests. It's the least I can do."

"You know, I didn't expect the students here to be helpful. I've heard a thing or three about the Fairbanks family. I'm surprised your school's participating in extramurals."

"It's Hal's dad. Ever since he took over, he's done all sorts of things differently. What do the Fairbanks have to do with it?"

"Mr. Fairbanks holds a seat on the school's Board of Trustees. Didn't you know?"

"Yeah." I winced. "I heard that. Mr. Pierce and Mrs. Onassis have similar views, but that's only three out of seven seats."

"I see." She grinned. "Do you know the headmaster's son? I mean, personally."

"Yes."

"I'd like to meet him if you have time to introduce us."

"He's probably in the infirmary right now. He goes there before breakfast, after lunch, and after dinner every day."

"Oh." The corners of her mouth turned down for the first time since I'd seen her. "Is he okay?"

"I'll let him answer that question." I sighed. "I'm not the gossipy type."

"I understand." She nodded.

"I've got it." Blaine held the book, beaming. "Would you mind terribly if I read it in here?"

"If you don't mind me going to visit with another student." Kim followed him to the table.

"Um." He glanced over his shoulder at the Ashfords, who nodded and smiled. "I suppose you can leave me in the care of these kind librarians for a little while."

"Peep!" Ember blinked sleepily for my shoulder, then crawled down my arm to get a better look at Blaine. "Peep?"

"I get to see your dragonet up close?" He grinned. "I never see them in Newport or even Providence. Mother doesn't like having them around, but there's no accounting for taste."

"Ember's one of two on campus." She flapped her wings, peeping and puffing her chest out proudly.

"She's adorable. I'll keep my eyes peeled for the other." He grinned. "Don't take too long, Kim."

"It'll take as long as it has to." She smiled, then leaned over and planted a kiss on the top of his head. "See you later."

We walked down the hall and out of the academic wing, and I pointed the way to the infirmary. I almost headed down with her when someone behind me cleared their throat.

"I guess I'll see you later too, Miss Morgenstern." Kim winced. "Thanks, and good luck."

Headmaster Hawkins stood behind me. He beckoned, and I followed him to his office. Inside were Professor DeBeer and Dylan, with Logan between them. I stopped in the doorway. The headmaster walked to his desk, sat down behind it, and picked up a pen.

"What's this about?" I asked.

"Mr. Khan tells me you knew he was an extramagus."

"Sort of. He said he was worried he might be one. I told him to talk to his professor, and he wrote a request for a meeting in the two-way notebook right after that."

"Did you see him attend such a meeting?"

"No." I shook my head. Dylan hung his. Gale rubbed against his cheek, chirping softly.

"I see." He wrote something on a paper.

"If you don't mind my asking, why?"

"I do mind, and I won't divulge further details until I've concluded my investigation."

"Oh. So," I said as I jerked my thumb at the door behind me, "I'll just be on my way."

"Have a seat, Miss Morgenstern. I'm not through with you yet."

I pulled up a chair and sat beside Dylan. Ember perched on my shoulder.

"I told you she had nothing to do with this." He protested. "You can't keep her here."

"Mr. Pierce." Headmaster Hawkins ignored Dylan's outburst. "Did you have any inkling that your roommate was an extramagus?"

"No." Doris leaped into Logan's lap, staring at the headmaster.

"It's unlikely." Professor DeBeer shook her head. "I'd expect anyone with his grades to notice something so unnatural."

"I'm still only a student." Logan peered at her. "Where's Professor Luciano? Shouldn't he be here?"

"Good question." The headmaster's face reminded me of a mahogany carving. "Irrelevant for now."

"What about Nurse Smith?" I clasped my hands together as Ember peeped. "He's got that lie-detector flask."

"It hasn't come to that yet. Miss Morgenstern, did you personally escort Mr. Khan to any faculty or staff member the day he told you his suspicions?"

"No. I only recommended meeting with his professor, which was what you said I should've done last year."

"Yes, that was my advice to you with regard to yourself."

I blinked. "You didn't mention other students."

"It's in the handbook, which you will read to me." He pushed a copy across the desk. "Page fifty-eight."

"Any student who witnesses extramagus activity must escort the suspected extramagus to a faculty member within two hours." I looked up after reading. "I'm sorry, I didn't know."

"Ignorance is no excuse, and since you're on probation, I expect you to get informed immediately after this meeting."

"Okay. But even though I didn't escort him, Dylan left the cafeteria, on his way to Professor DeBeer. Did that meeting not happen?"

"Professor, did Dylan Khan meet with you to discuss that he might be an extramagus?"

"No, headmaster. He made an appointment but didn't show."

The pit of my stomach dropped. I couldn't imagine Dylan would lie about that, not to me.

She hates our kind and would just as soon see us all locked up, even if we've done nothing wrong.

"Mr. Khan, for the last time. Did you meet with Professor DeBeer that day?"

"Yes. I went straight to her office. I skipped practice with Coach Pickman, even, and I definitely told her."

"I didn't see him all afternoon." Logan shook his head. "Anyone in our year would say the same thing. Headmaster, there's got to be another explanation."

"Absence is no alibi." The headmaster sighed. "Someone is lying, and the only person with a motive is your roommate. So once more, Miss Morgenstern. Did you witness Mr. Khan approach either of your professors on the day in question?"

"No. He was headed for the academic wing, though." I shook my head. "I saw Temperance Fairbanks walking the same way. Logan's right, there's got to be another explanation. Could somebody have interfered?"

"There are no mind magi on campus. Mental tampering is outside the realm of possibility. For now, I must consider the simplest explanation true. Mr. Khan, you're suspended from extracurricular activities until we test the full scope of your abilities."

"I understand, sir." He closed his eyes.

"You're all dismissed."

Logan and I stood, waiting for Dylan, who was not okay. I couldn't blame him. He already felt like an outsider, and now he couldn't play Bishop's Row until he'd passed whatever test the headmaster had mentioned.

"That includes you, Professor." He stood, placing his hands on the surface of his desk. "I need time alone with my files and thoughts."

"But Headmaster, extracurricular suspension isn't enough. He should be removed from campus."

"Dismissed, Professor. Unless you want to be removed from my office magically."

"Fine." She stood, then sauntered past us, tossing a glare at Dylan as she went. Her lightning bird turned his head, cawing back at us through the door.

We hustled out but gave the professor space. The last thing I wanted was to make the adult magus angrier. In the lobby, Dylan made a beeline for the café, where he went behind the counter and grabbed an apron. He withdrew into serving customers like a turtle into its shell.

Logan and I stared at each other, dumbstruck. His eyes looked shiny, and I knew from the heat at the corners of mine that both of us were about to cry. We awkwardly exchanged goodbyes, and he headed upstairs while I wandered around the lobby like a lost puppy.

CHAPTER ELEVEN

"Come lounge in the lounge with us."

Cadence stood over me as I sat on the bench in the lobby. We'd barely spoken since the visiting students had arrived on campus. I felt guilty for spending an hour with Izzy without her, so I went.

Hawthorn Academy students all wore identical blazers over bland yet generally high- quality clothing. Kids from Messing, while quirky, wore green and gray uniforms accessorized and accented in high vintage beatnik style. The Gallows Hill crew was another breed entirely.

The usually sedate and quiet lounge was a riot of bright colors and raucous sounds. Cadence's school didn't do uniforms. I didn't realize that went beyond the clothing on their backs.

The diversity at Gallows Hill made all the difference. I froze in place with my mouth wide open. Even my experience in mundane schools hadn't prepared me for their student body.

They laughed louder, smiled brighter, and shared personal space to a degree I reserved for family and close friends. One glance around the room told me that most of the Hawthorn and Messing students had decided to congregate elsewhere. I could understand how Michelina, Eston, or Logan might find this scene off-putting. I almost left because I'd grown accustomed to quiet here.

I spotted Noah off in the far corner. He sat with Elanor, yukking it up over a game of Uno. I didn't want to be shown up by my big brother, and Cadence was one of those aforementioned close friends, so I stuck around and got punched in the shoulder for my trouble.

"Hey, I remember you," a voice to my right rumbled. Ember looked up without any hint of alarm, so I turned my head toward the speaker.

The guy was tall and way more muscular than most seventeen-year-olds, which made sense. He was a changeling, powerful enough for me to feel the glamour coming off him. I realized where we'd met before.

"The Night Creatures concert, right?" I nodded. "I'm Aliyah."

"Yeah, the veterinarian's kid." He was talking about my father, who worked with mundane animals in a community clinic across town when he wasn't helping Bubbe. "I'm Bar."

"Is that a nickname?"

"Haven't gone by my official name for ages." He grunted, jerking his chin at Ember. "Haven't seen one of those in almost as long."

"Like, literal ages?" I raised an eyebrow. Most changelings grew up in the regular world but some spent time in the Under, where they aged more slowly. Bar might have been around for decades.

"That's personal."

"Okay." I shrugged.

"Be nice." Cadence's voice took on a more lilting tone than usual. "We're all going to get along, have a laugh, sing a song."

I instantly relaxed, like I was alone on the beach in the sun instead of in a crowd of strangers.

"Whatever you say, boss lady." Bar nodded and ambled off, joining a group of what could only be wolf shifters on the big sofa by the wall.

"You didn't just whammy us, Cadence?" I blinked, shaking off the unexpected calm. "We were having a conversation."

"It's officially my job. I'm part of the Safety Squad." She pointed at a pin on her shirt. "The principal picked three of us to keep rowdy students in line. She takes this visit seriously, for good reason."

Cadence looped her arm through my elbow, escorting me to the corner opposite Noah's. Her classmates watched as she smiled and waved like we were on a parade float. Almost all went back to the business of loudly socializing, except for Brianna Collins, who continued watching us.

"Is Brianna on the Safety Squad?"

"Yup, and Azrael, but I don't know where he went off to." She shrugged. "Anyway, the Safety Squad's not why I want to talk. Is Dylan really an extramagus?"

"Yeah, and the worst part is, I've known since our first week back. And now he's in trouble with the headmaster."

"What happened?"

I told her the whole crazy story, including the case of the missing meeting.

"You need Izzy. Find out what she sees for Dylan, if anything."

"What do you mean, 'if anything?'"

"She has a hard time reading for you, didn't you know?"

"I've never seen that happen."

"Not when you're there, silly." Cadence giggled, her voice pitched at a register I knew meant she was nervous. "She can't get an accurate read remotely on you. After you got solar magic, she pulled cards when you weren't there, and they said gobbledygook. She thinks it's because you're an extramagus."

"She might be right." I shook my head. "Maybe Dylan will agree to a reading in person if he ever gets out from behind that counter."

"That sucks. I can't believe his professor." She shook her head. "You watched him ask for a meeting in that notebook. She must be lying."

"That's the thing, Cadence. I'm not sure who to believe."

"Dylan, of course." She clicked her tongue. "Was she hard on him before today?"

"I don't think so, but he's been out of sorts all month."

"Relationship problems do that. He's probably not over Grace. Anyway, I'm on Team Dylan, not Team DeBeer."

"She totally surprised me with her attitude about extramagi." I sighed. "I thought she was a cool professor."

"Maybe there's no such thing as a cool professor." Cadence shrugged. "Teachers aren't here to be our friends. They make sure we learn everything we need and prepare us for life out there." She waved a hand vaguely at the exit hall. "Angels ferrying knowledge up from the inky depths, they are not."

"You have no idea what angels are like for us." I snorted. "In the stories Dad and Bubbe tell, they're terrifying, full of snap judgments and immutable messages. A lot like professors, actually."

"I get it. Your angels are like our demons, diving in to drop nets on our heads."

"Yeah, that's pretty much the vibe."

"Anyway, I met Dorian Spanos earlier. He's interesting."

I sighed. "I wish he and Dylan could just get along. Maybe they'll do it for Logan."

"Oh, yeah, Logan's got it bad," Cadence said, chuckling. "But it looks like someone else is on the sweet romance diabetes train."

She jerked her thumb at the other corner, where Noah now stood, shifting his weight from one foot to the other. I hadn't seen him that nervous since the night middle school put on *Little Shop of Horrors*.

"Whoa." I blinked.

Jonah smiled like a movie star, but with fangs. The way he tilted his head as he spoke made me think he'd asked a question I couldn't hear over the Gallows Hill students. Whatever it was made Elanor clap her hands and bounce in her seat. Noah blushed profusely, nodding.

"Did he just ask him out?" Cadence squeezed my arm. "That's only the cutest thing ever!"

"Not around here. We've got serious vampire haters on this campus, remember?"

"Oh, my God, they're holding hands. Noah doesn't care about any of that."

I watched them leave the lounge, heading toward the lobby. I wondered how Dylan was, hiding behind his work.

Go and find out. You never know what might happen.

"I don't want to know." I put my hand over my mouth. "Sorry, Cadence."

"I'm cool with your inside voice." Cadence relaxed her grip on my arm, patting it. "Sorry, I got a little excited."

"How do you feel about being here? Honesty time."

"It's exciting but stressful. Safety Squad's like herding cats, figuratively. Most of them aren't feline, just the tag-along." She jerked her thumb at a boy I'd seen on the beach before school started.

"Who's that?"

"Cosmo, Blaine Harcourt's godson. He's only here for the Magipsych Fair. At least he behaves himself, unlike other people." She narrowed her eyes, flaring her nostrils at a lanky guy roughhousing with Bar. I'd also seen him before, but mostly, I'd heard his voice while hiding behind a crate with Grace.

"Who's that?" I knew his name but not what Cadence thought of him.

"Oh, Crow? He's nobody, um, important." Her face turned beet-red, and she flipped stray curls of auburn hair over her shoulder. "He and Bar have been friends for ages, kind of like us with Izzy."

"Why do I get the impression you're not telling me the whole story?"

And you're not telling her what you heard Crow doing at the Lyceum. Why is that?

"We've dated. A few times." Her eyes moved from side to side like a nonexistent ping-pong match was happening on my shoulders.

"Wait a minute. Isn't he a bird shifter? Are you telling me a mermaid and a bird have an on-again-off-again relationship?"

"You're taking it way better than my parents did." She shrugged. "Anyway, our relationship status is subject to change."

"Aren't you worried it's too much like oil and vinegar?"

"Oil and vinegar is the stuff of amazing salad dressings," Cadence said, smirking.

I couldn't argue with that, and her nonsensical quip cheered me up. I found myself laughing despite the campus feeling like a powder keg.

"That's the Aliyah Morgenstern I know and love." Cadence patted my shoulder.

"She's been in short supply lately." I sighed. "Thanks, Cadence."

"Any time." She grinned. "Hey, I know you'll be in and out for Yom Kippur this week, but are you going home for Sukkot after that?"

"Yeah, to build the Sukkah, and also for the hour during sunset all that week. They let us off-campus for weekday religious holidays. Did you want to celebrate with us?"

"If it's no trouble, could I have an open invitation?"

"Of course."

After that, she introduced me around. The Gallows Hill wildness wasn't as scary close-up. Instead, it was their version of warmth and welcome and how they communicated with each other and their surroundings. I understood why Cadence loved her classmates enough to take responsibility for them.

Elanor made a quiet exit, and Noah returned with Jonah and a pot of tea. I almost went over to say hello, but they were totally engrossed in each other. I didn't want to interrupt the one nice thing to happen that day.

Yawning reminded me to check the time. There were only twenty minutes before lights out. I made my goodbyes, then headed upstairs to change into pajamas before falling into bed. Grace was asleep when I got there.

CHAPTER TWELVE

The next afternoon at lunch, the PA system summoned me to the office.

Headmaster Hawkins stood with his back to me in front of his bookcase, hands behind his back. I recognized his posture as a sign of the inner turmoil I'd seen after Hal's diagnosis last spring, but his voice sounded more monotone than it had on that occasion.

"Good afternoon, Miss Morgenstern. You must wonder why you're here."

"Yes, sir, I do." I took a seat in front of his desk beside Professor Luciano, who'd been there when I arrived.

"I've requested your assistance as Dylan Khan's friend and peer." He turned and sat. "We're testing the scope of his abilities tomorrow. You must agree not to discuss this with anyone besides the involved parties and your immediate family."

"Okay, I agree." I folded my hands in my lap, knuckles bone-white. "But why not ask Logan?"

"Mr. Pierce will supervise your classmates while they remain in the library tomorrow during your usual lab period."

"Where will you be, Professor?" I blinked.

"Escorting you and Dylan to the test," Professor Luciano said.

Headmaster Hawkins answered before I could ask my question. "Regulations require an instructor's presence, and Professor DeBeer declined." He bowed his head briefly, revealing the puffiness under his eyes. I heard a noise and felt a rush of air behind me.

"Where are his parents?"

"I'm standing in for them."

"Mom?" I turned, eyes widening as I watched my mother straighten her jacket. The headmaster must have teleported her.

"Extramagus testing is rigorous, unforgiving, and not without safety risks." She sat in the third chair, on the other side of me. "I'm acting as a guardian on his behalf. This form bears his father's signature. "

"This isn't fair." I crossed my arms over my chest. "Why didn't I go through this last year?"

"Last year, we didn't have an unsolved poisoning." Headmaster Hawkins leveled his gaze at me. "If there was unexplained sabotage here last spring, you'd have endured the same process."

"I don't like it."

"Nobody does." Professor Luciano sighed. His strix leaned on his head, pushing his glasses askew. He didn't seem to mind.

"Four of the seven trustees requested further investigation," Headmaster Hawkins said. "It's either this test under my jurisdiction on campus or adding Dylan to the list of suspects on file with Salem PD. They'd detain him for questioning."

"Nurse Smith will be there, right?" I sniffled, blinking rapidly. "Since it's dangerous, I mean."

"Yes, though the risks aren't merely medical. Miss Ichiro and Mr. Harcourt have offered their services in case of an emergency. "

"What good will a dragon and a tanuki do?" I stood, placing my hands palm-down on the desk.

"We haven't covered magical shifters yet, Miss Morgenstern." Professor Luciano patted one of my hands. "Rest assured, those two are uniquely qualified to reduce the risk in this ordeal."

I wasn't reassured, not after he called it an ordeal. I dropped my hands to my sides, but I didn't get back in my seat like a good little student.

"Fine, I'll go. But only for Dylan's sake. If you'll excuse me, I've got to eat something before Bishop's Row practice."

As I paced toward the door, my mother gave me an approving nod. Last year I would've wondered why all day, but I understood her better now. Mom stuck to the rules, but she wasn't afraid to use the system to change unfair ones.

At practice, I stood at mid-court with Lee, where I could get the tension out of my body if not off my mind. Dylan sat on the bench with Faith, watching. He'd been switched to reserves instead of taken off the team entirely, pending his results. Coach Pickman didn't want to replace him. If poison was one of his magical elements, Alex would end up taking his place.

At lunch, he came right out and said so to my face. I'd brushed it off, but the anger festered, so I overdid my next fire orb by a country mile.

"Rein it in, Aliyah!" Elanor hollered behind me. "Let's keep our eyebrows!"

"Sorry." I tried banishing the big fire energy between my hands, which shrank but turned a much hotter blue.

"Time out!" Coach Pickman's whistle cleared the court. "Morgenstern, deep breathing exercises now! The rest of you run laps."

"This sucks." Noah glared as he ran past. Lee jogged behind him, shrugging.

"Said I was sorry." I sat on the court's hardwood floor to begin my breathing exercises. I even closed my eyes but didn't have much success relaxing.

"Come on, you can do this." Elanor made like a good team captain and sat across from me, reaching her hands out to take mine. "We're fire, so it's hard for us to chill. Plus, you're related to Noah, so I expect you to be over the top sometimes."

"Thanks." This time instead of closing my eyes, I stared at our interlaced fingers. A tingle of energy passed between us. "Are you banishing?"

"Uh-huh." She nodded. "After what Logan said you did in Lab last year, I'm surprised you're having trouble banishing over a year later."

"There's too much going on."

"Like there wasn't last year?" She raised an eyebrow. "Charity was a megabitch. Every day feels like vacation since she graduated."

"I'd trade the stuff happening now to deal with her again instead."

"I wouldn't." She shook her head. "She was a powder keg. Tempe is too, but Grace has her checked better socially than I ever managed with Charity. Thank goodness Faith is the black sheep of that family."

"Last year, familiars didn't get hurt. How did you do it?"

"Performance art." She shrugged. "Improv. Guess I'm decent at playing pretend."

"I'm not. I worry about everybody. I need to keep them safe."

"That's not your job description."

"I'm not sure what is." I sighed, finally feeling my fire bank down.

"And you think I do?" One corner of her mouth turned up. "It's not your job to save the world, Morgenstern."

Maybe she wouldn't say that if she knew the whole story.

Coach Pickman blew her whistle again. I managed to get through practice without burning the gym down. I tried to follow Dylan afterward since I wanted to ask him about the next day's testing, but he was nowhere to be found.

Because of the High Holidays, I went to my room, skipping dinner since Yom Kippur meant fasting after sundown. Tired and hungry, I took a bath, got into pajamas, and listened to music to pass the time. I fell asleep before Grace returned to our room.

The next morning I could barely pay attention at Lecture, so I made use of our magical notebooks to keep track. I could always study later, at home after Yom Kippur services and dinner. I found it ironic that

Dylan's test came on my religion's day of atonement. He'd be judged for something he couldn't help, and if he failed, he wouldn't get a chance to make up for it.

When Lecture let out, we left Ember and Gale in the infirmary with Nurse Smith, who put them into the cart that housed unbound critters during Familiar Bonding. They peered at us, Ember peeping incessantly and Gale rattling the wire around the enclosure. Nurse Smith crooned something at them as we walked out.

Professor Luciano led Dylan and me all the way down the hall in the academic wing. The section past the library hadn't been used since long before Noah's first year at Hawthorn. A few classrooms were occupied by Gallows Hill and Messing students. I saw Izzy through one of the windows, eyes wide and eyebrows raised as she watched us file by. I couldn't have told her or Cadence about it anyway.

At the end of the hall stood a set of double doors, fitted with stained glass like the ones in the lobby. I'd never seen these before. Professor Luciano stopped and stared, one hand on the latch, pinned in place like a butterfly to a card, transfixed.

The artwork was striking, no doubt. Red and orange flames flickered above a landscape of purple ice, tinged blue where the firelight touched it. Somehow, the ice and fire together created a heat more intense than the inferno I'd banished last year. It was terrifying and beautiful at the same time, the art even more masterful than the glass on the other door.

That didn't explain why it had so much impact on our professor. He was faculty, so surely he'd seen it before. I almost wished the Evil Inside Voice would chime in and throw me some trivia about this mural, but it was silent about the art.

"*Fire and Ice?*" Dylan read the title, then shook his head. "Impossible."

I died a little inside. Only the Evil Inside Voice noticed.

What did you expect?

"Why do you say that?" I cleared my throat, wishing I hadn't sounded quite so strangled.

"It's by a Morgenstern in 1979. That was before your grandma's time, but after her parents."

"It's by her late brother." Professor Luciano's voice was low-pitched and quavered. "His name was Noah."

"How did you know about my great-uncle?" The professor didn't reply or even bother looking at me, but his strix did.

Her head turned all the way around, and she blinked at me twice. I wondered what that meant until the strix trilled in the voice she used to calm other critters. She pressed her head against my temple and tried to help me understand. It hurt the professor to look at me, but the reason was either lost in translation or a mystery to the professor's familiar.

"Why's the ice purple?" Dylan shook his head. "It looks like poison. Still impossible."

"We are the masters of untold elemental forces, Mr. Khan. More things are possible with love and magic than not, beyond imagining for some, at the edge of memory for unfortunate others."

With that cryptic sentiment, Professor Luciano pulled the door open, holding it as we walked through. I glanced up to see his eyes watery, focused on something far away in either distance or time. Possibly both.

CHAPTER THIRTEEN

The doors led into an auditorium, where the fresh scents of wood soap and polish permeated the air. The entire place had recently been cleaned, likely for the talent show after Thanksgiving. But while the stage lights were up and the curtains open, only one row of seats stood in the front, with two chairs empty.

That Board of Trustees, no doubt.

We arrived last. None of the seven trustees, my mother, or the headmaster had prior commitments that day. What caught me by surprise was the iron dais on the stage. It wasn't just a platform, though. As we approached, light reflected off the clear sides of an enclosure around it.

Whether it was made of glass, crystal, or something else, I didn't know. Dylan found out, because Nurse Smith led him up to it, opened a panel at the back, and locked him inside. My mother had grossly understated things, calling this process rigorous.

It looked downright draconian. Locking anyone in a cage was wrong, extramagus with unknown powers or not.

You don't know the half of it, my sweet summer child.

The Evil Inside Voice never made a physical sound, but my mind usually perceived it as a drolly sarcastic baritone. Now it seemed

111

throaty and hushed. I couldn't fathom what was different just then, how it could carry more than the vague foreboding sitting in my gut. Wasn't the voice part of my brain? Didn't it come from me, some fragment of personality given autonomy by the extra power flowing across the barrier between my body and Faerie's Under?

"Aliyah, take a seat, please." My mother patted the arm of the chair next to her.

I sat between her and Blaine Harcourt. I couldn't muster happiness at seeing him again or a greeting. His presence was ancillary to Dylan's plight, and all of my mental and emotional energy focused on my friend. That was my charge, my reason for being here: as his peer and witness.

One thing was missing, something I should have realized. Somebody had to administer the test, and though I knew little about it, no individual present had authority with the Extrahuman Registry. Headmaster Hawkins rose from his seat, then turned to face the rest of us with his back to the stage's apron.

"Ladies and gentlemen, to ensure this process follows guidelines set forth by the United States and by extension the International Registry, I invite Director-General Rockport of the New England Regional Extrahuman Registry branch."

I almost turned around to look back through the door I'd come in by. If I had, I would've missed the director's entrance from stage left. He must've waited in the wings all that time, watching everyone arrive.

Instead of addressing us or even acknowledging the existence of an audience, Director-General Rockport paced across the stage with his eyes on Dylan. A charcoal suit covered his tall, rangy body, but it did nothing to diminish the wolfishness of his frame. A fringe of salt-and-pepper hair ringed his otherwise-bald head. His expression was so neutral, I couldn't determine his age. I made a mental note to ask Cadence if he'd ever shown up in the social papers.

Blaine Harcourt tightened his right hand on the arm between our seats. The wood creaked, which made me nervous. If a powerful dragon shifter who could take on a form the size of a football field was scared of this guy, Dylan was in serious trouble, and I couldn't help him. This was a test of his elements and abilities as an extramagus. Interference might force him to repeat the entire process.

"It's okay, Blaine." Kim put her hand over his, but it trembled. After their fingers interlaced, their knuckles went white.

I blinked, unsure what had them on edge. And then I remembered that dragon shifters could see magical energy and tanukis could see the flow of luck. Was it the box that frightened them or Dylan? Or him being inside it? Did Director-General Rockport inspire all that terror?

Be glad you're seated beside your mother.

"I am."

"I will brook no comments from witnesses." The director spoke without turning to face me, but his words hit like a blow to the stomach.

He reached for his interior jacket pocket and produced a pair of metallic spectacles. I sensed they weren't ordinary, but before I got a good look, he put them on, his head obscuring them from view. After that, he put his left hand in his outside pocket. I watched it move under the fabric. The iron and glass box on stage made a noise.

It sounded like the air conditioning compressor outside Bubbe's office. As Dylan's eyes widened with alarm and his hands went up to his neck, I understood. The Director was creating a vacuum in there.

"Use your registered element," he said in an impossibly level monotone. How could any sentient person address another so calmly in a situation this dire? How many times had he done this?

Trust me, you don't want to know.

Dylan set his jaw and responded instead of panicking further. He raised his hands like a mime pressing against an invisible ceiling, then I watched him open his mouth and practically gulp in the air he created around himself. The compressor noise stopped and the director nodded, his hand moving in his pocket again.

"Now, the temperature rises."

This time Dylan nodded, expecting what was coming. I breathed a premature sigh of relief, confident he'd keep cool.

But either he was too unaccustomed to ice magic, or he lacked confidence. It had taken me months to control solar, so I couldn't blame him, especially with how his school year had gone so far. This test was designed to be rigorous, challenging, and exacting. And worse, as it turned out.

Admit it. This is pure cruelty.

I watched as the clear enclosure glowed red. The Director even pulled a handkerchief from somewhere and dabbed his forehead with it. Sweat beaded on Dylan's brow, but finally, he managed the concentration to call on his second element. Rockport nodded again, adjusting whatever control hid in his pocket.

"Additional element ice, confirmed. Now, the temperature drops."

The process repeated with a new element. Did he intend to run him through the entire gamut of magic elements? How could anyone consider this test within humane parameters? Was it new since the Reveal or something that had been in use for ages? How many extra-magi had they done this to? Dylan shivered until his teeth chattered, but nothing happened. Before long, that segment ended.

"Fire element negative. And now, darkness."

I felt numb, detached from everything. Everybody still saw Dylan; nothing looked different to the witnesses. But his eyes went wide and wild, and he wrapped his arms around himself, seeming to shrink in fear from nothing.

Being immersed in impenetrable darkness was a primal fear, one shared by most sentient beings on the planet other than vampires, Umbral Magi, and their kindred critters. But none of us had to endure that terror today, only Dylan.

I glanced down the line of people, four of whom I'd never seen. I recognized Mrs. Onassis, Mr. Pierce, and Mr. Fairbanks. They yawned like Dylan was up there method-acting instead of being punished.

Punishment for being what he is? Horrific.

I'd promised to be his witness, so I couldn't look away. Dylan quaked and quivered in there, terrified but unable to mitigate the absence of light around him. I grasped my mother's hand.

"How long?"

"Another minute." My mother laced her fingers through mine and squeezed. I wished I could get into her lap and curl up there the way I had as a small child, but I was seventeen, and a formal witness for an official Registry test. And an extramagus. No comfort could erase my horror at this cruel procedure. It shouldn't have been an approved global standard for anybody, even Uncle Richard.

"Make it stop." Blaine trembled in his seat, shoulders hunched.

Kim put her arm around him. "Ten seconds."

That small humane act made me feel impossibly guilty. Someone should have been here for him. Not as a witness in a chair, but inside the box beside Dylan, so he wasn't alone. Maybe a shifter or a psychic. Why wasn't that allowed?

"Solar element negative. And now, light."

Who does he think he is, God? Lucifer, more like.

Dylan covered his eyes with his hands, fruitlessly from the way he screamed. This was not a test. It was torture and utterly inhumane. That was why the Registry didn't designate a support extrahuman inside the box.

I'd go through this exact ordeal in less than a year. Everyone with more than one magical element had to, suspicion of crime or not. No wonder Uncle Richard had lied about his abilities.

I'd grown up in Salem and had known the history of witch-trials here for as long as I could remember. Never in my wildest dreams could I have imagined they still existed in an internationally-sanctioned form for any percentage of magi.

"Umbral element negative."

The test progressed, and yes, Director Rockport went through every magical element known to extrahumanity. He ended by testing for the rarest ability in existence, mind magic.

"Now, Mr. Khan, ask to be released without using your voice or body language."

Dylan leaned his forehead against the front of his prison. The tawny skin of his brow was pressed flat and his eyes were closed. Every one of us watched tears pour out, roll down his face, and splash against his already sweat-stained shirt. His hands balled into fists at his sides, and that small act of defiance guillotined my last scrap of composure.

I no longer felt far-off or detached, instead breaking into a series of wet sobs that shook the entire row of chairs, along with my body. My limbs felt stiff and weak all at the same time, my face blazing like the sun, feet as frigid and heavy as blocks of ice.

The seven Trustees at the other end of the row leaned forward to peer at me. One, a very elderly man I didn't know with a thick white beard, sniffled and wiped away a tear. The fox in his lap whined.

Mom had her arm around me, but it did no good. She couldn't offer me any comfort. She could never understand how horrifying this was, watching my friend, already in anguish, endure even more. Knowing I'd be in his place soon enough.

Kim Ichiro got it. Not caring one bit what anybody thought, the tanuki rose from her seat and ushered me out of mine, leading me off to the side and giving me a bear hug I wouldn't have thought possible from someone so short and slight.

"This is the most horrible thing I've ever seen in my life," she whispered in my ear. "My father's a lawyer, and I'm telling him everything. This can't continue."

"Even after Richard Hopewell?" I managed.

"Especially after Richard Hopewell." She patted my back. "He was terrible, but we have to do better than this."

Finally, it was over. In the end, Dylan had aptitude for only the two elements he'd initially admitted to. They could've taken his word for it, but either the system distrusted us or considered us too mentally unstable to give an accurate accounting of our abilities.

Dylan and I might have been born with extra magical power, but the world did its best to make sure we had plenty of other disadvantages.

CHAPTER FOURTEEN

We went to Yom Kippur service in Beverly, the same as every year. Crossing the bridge felt different, heavier somehow. On the way there and during the service, I wanted forgiveness more than ever.

At first, I wasn't sure what I'd done wrong, but failure to act hurt others as much as direct harm. I wanted to take a stand and change how extramagi were treated, but it all felt hollow and false because I hadn't spoken out about it.

When the shofar blew, my heart opened along with my mind and cleared away all fear of what my family might think. There was something I could say, maybe even something to do.

The idea couldn't change the past, but it could help tip the balance toward equity for extramagi. I couldn't change the system, but maybe I could expose it.

The ride back over the bridge into Salem felt like hours instead of minutes. When we went upstairs and prepared to break our fast, the last thing on my mind was food despite how good all the dishes looked, how amazing they smelled, how hungry I was. No drop of drink or crumb of food would pass between my lips, not until I told my family about my plan.

"Mom. Dad. Bubbe. I'm taking that test." They paused, hands over chairs, a pitcher poised over the glass in my father's hand—my family, frozen in time. Noah broke the spell.

"What do you mean?" He scratched his head. "Exams aren't until spring, Aliyah."

"Not that." I looked at Mom, pinning her gaze with mine. "You know what I mean. The extramagus test. The one Dylan took today."

"Wait." Noah blinked. "They test extrama—"

"No."

I whirled, startled by Bubbe's voice behind me. The tray of babka in her hand sagged, nearly tipping over. I rushed to her side and set it on the counter, then I put my hands on my hips and planted my feet in front of her.

"No?" My nostrils flared.

"You heard me. There's no way you're taking that test until you have to, Aliyah." Bubbe narrowed her eyes. Her hair, cobalt blue this time, trembled. Was she angry or scared? For what felt like the second worst moment of my life, I realized I didn't care.

That's not true. You care too much. That's always your problem.

"I'm way more dangerous in a wooden school than a boy with ice and air." My voice cracked. "I want Mom to call Director-General Rockport tomorrow, and then I'll take that test."

"What you want is irrelevant, child." Bubbe looked over my head at my parents. "Neither of you will consent to this foolishness. It's out of the question."

I turned slowly, measuring my movement because I didn't want to see what I knew would be there: resignation on both my parents' faces.

"You're right, Mom," Dad agreed reluctantly.

"I'm glad you said that, Aaron." My mother put her hand to her throat, her only tell when frightened. "I'm in total agreement with Bubbe. Minor extramagi need parental consent. That rule's in place for a reason. I won't give mine in a million years. And if you do, Aaron, so help me—"

"I hear you both," Dad said, "but my uncle took it as an adult. The love of his life volunteered just like this when he was younger than

Aliyah is now. In June, she'll have to take it. The test is the only way for extramagi."

"It shouldn't be." I crossed my arms over my chest.

"If that's how you feel, Aliyah, why push?" Noah shuddered. "I don't know jack, but that fucking thing sounds catastrophic."

"Noah, language!" Mom made a zipping motion over her lips. He winced and hung his head.

"It looks like evil to me, and torture is wrong. I want them to test me in public, so everyone knows how bad it is. To make it stop."

"You're not responsible for every extramagi on this Earth." Bubbe stepped forward and put her hand on my shoulder. Her tone softened, but her eyes remained hard and angry. "My brother's powers came in at age twenty, and that test made him suffer every day. What do you think will happen to you?" She sighed. "This isn't revolution, it's self-harm. You're not Moses. You're Jacob, and we're refusing to be Isaac."

"I'm Judah, lighting a lamp." My throat tightened. Ember wrapped around my shoulders, her tail pressed against my cheek. "The test is desecration. If magi have to see it, they'll know we need another way."

"You're still a minor," Bubbe insisted.

"I'm not giving up on this plan."

"You will until you're eighteen and we can't protect you any longer. I was my brother's witness." Bubbe pressed her fingertips to her breastbone. "I sat in your place and saw what you saw, and I've tried to change it all this time because I love you all so much. I failed. What makes you think you'll succeed?"

"Bubbe, I know how hard you can fight." My eyes overflowed. "But you're not an extramagus."

"Is that supposed to mean I don't understand?" Her fingertips paled against her white shirt.

"No, you get it, but you can't speak for a group you're not part of, Bubbe. Not for something like this."

"I only exist because enough gentiles stood up for Jews during the Shoah, Bissel." She sighed. "Like everyone else in this room."

"This test doesn't happen where people can see, but caring for one person is the key to opening your heart. All they know about us is

Richard Hopewell in an orange jumpsuit. I'm asking you to let me be seen."

"She's got that part right." Dad nodded.

"Then go on the news." Noah shrugged. "Do an interview with Cadence's mom. Make a viral video. Mom and Bubbe almost never freak out about the same thing. Maybe they're right."

"Noah has good ideas here. Other ways to raise awareness." Mom put her arm around my brother. I stared, wondering why nobody did the same for me.

They're afraid. You're incandescent.

I looked at my hands. The Evil Inside Voice was right. I glowed with a light too orange for pure solar magic. I'd conjured both elements without realizing it. I'd never hurt my family, but they didn't seem to believe that.

"Peep." Ember craned her neck around to look me in the eye, then reached out with one claw and stroked the bridge of my nose, the way I did with her when she was upset. At least she wasn't afraid.

She's on your side, always.

I turned on my heel and ran upstairs, slamming the door to my room before banging my head on the sloped ceiling. I fell into bed sickened and weeping and curled up around Ember. Even the aroma of Bubbe's chocolate babka turned my stomach.

Eventually, I had to use the bathroom. Outside my door, I found a plate piled with food, a sign of love. Too bad what I needed that day was their support.

CHAPTER FIFTEEN

The next day, Dylan replaced Bailey in Professor Luciano's homeroom. Bailey had gone to DeBeer's class with her sister. I waved as he entered the room, pointing at the seat between Logan and me.

Dylan sat in the back, head down over his notebook as the professor gave his lecture. He wasn't alone since Hal came in right after him and took the seat beside him. Faith made her way to the front and sat with us.

I had a hard time concentrating for the second day in a row, for more than one reason. That afternoon we'd be in the magipsychic lab with our teams, working on our projects for the fair. My brain moved a mile a minute on other things besides Axis and Allied magi during the Second World War.

Maybe you're just avoiding uncomfortable subject matter.

I shook my head and activated the book's auto-notes, then doodled in the margins. I'd want to look over more detailed notes later than what I could manage taking now.

"Rumors of shifter and faerie activity during the war became the stuff of foxhole folklore. Magi kept their involvement on more subtle terms. The Allies had magi working in secret as munitions designers, but the Axis magi were more ambitious. If they'd cared more about advancing the mundane Axis cause, Allied forces would have lost the Second World War."

Too close to home for your family.

I couldn't ignore the reactions from my classmates, whose gasps carried through the room. Only Dylan seemed unimpressed, likely because the UK had endured direct attacks on their soil. Although misery loves company, I hoped their stomachs didn't turn as much as mine did. If the Axis had won, I'd never have been born.

Don't go making assumptions now.

"What?"

"Miss Morgenstern, if you're having trouble hearing from the front row, I'm not sure what other accommodation to give you." Professor Luciano turned from his chalk drawing. "However, it is vital that you absorb the lecture from this point forward. It's of extreme importance."

"Sorry about the outburst, Professor."

"Let us continue, then.

"Only the most specialized of educators would be able to tell you that Axis magi were distracted by one specific obsession. I happen to be one of two in the know at this hallowed institution."

Logan put his hand up and spoke after Professor Luciano nodded.

"Who's the other?"

"He's unable to teach here despite holding numerous degrees, but you all know Ezekiel Brown. His knowledge comes first-hand from occupying an Axis magipsychic research base at the end of the war. In a chamber beneath the basement level, he found this."

He completed a chalkboard picture, then stepped aside so we could see it. Instead of troops in uniform, bombers in flight, or a bombed-out countryside, he'd depicted a device I'd never forget after the previous day's events: the glass and iron dais used in the test.

A loud wooden clattering sounded behind me. Dylan had stood, and his chair had toppled behind him. Gale flapped in the air above his head.

"How many?" He pointed at the board. "How many extramagi did they torture? How many died?"

"Nobody counted them. Even today we're not sure, but estimates are in the thousands."

I raised my hand, and he acknowledged it.

"Why isn't this widely known?"

"It's a complex answer. The forces occupying the base couldn't determine what the device was for until much later. They had to keep it secret from their mundane allies. But in the sixties, when it became apparent to our society that a reveal would happen, extrahumans with influence took pains to investigate the Axis records and this device, along with several others in storage. Once we needed a Registry, we had enough magipsychic technology to create our own regulatory organization. The rest is public relations, designed to ensure peace between humans and extrahumans."

"Why didn't they count the extramagi?" Faith asked without raising her hand. "The Axis murdered them just like they did mundanes. Didn't the Allied magi care?"

"I'm afraid they did care, Miss Fairbanks, but for the wrong reasons. The Allies stopped the war, but they were flawed." He looked over our heads. "Do you need a break, Mr. Khan?"

"No." He shook his head, then beckoned to Gale, who landed on his shoulder again. "No, I think I'll be okay hearing this from you, sir."

"Here." Hal righted the seat, and Dylan murmured a word of thanks before sitting back down in it.

The lecture continued, eventually concluding with a list of related books in the library. In Creatives, Dylan immediately got his guitar and sat in the corner, tapping the strings instead of strumming them. I understood he needed to play but didn't want to distract everybody else. All the talk of horrible magipsychic devices had jogged my memory about some of the more beneficial ones.

I got permission and headed down to the library to get something. The Ashfords nodded and smiled, giving me no trouble when I requested the item be checked out under Dylan's name instead of mine. When I returned to Creatives, I headed to him.

"Give these a try." I held the item out to him.

"This guitar's acoustic, so I don't see how headphones will help. Nice thought, though."

"It's magipsychic Bluetooth. Let me show you."

He nodded, so I slipped the headphones over his ears, then took the guitar from him. I held the body to one side and the fretboard to the other while imagining sound moving from the instrument to the headset, then I handed the guitar back to him.

"Give it a try."

He strummed a chord, and his mouth dropped open. He looked up at me, blinking. I smiled.

"Do you like it?"

"How did you know about this miracle?"

"Noah uses something like that at home when he plays bass, but they work with any instrument."

"Wow." He gave me a half-smile. "You're a lifesaver."

"Nah, I just got them from the library."

"It's a huge improvement for practicing. Thanks, Aliyah."

"I'll leave you to it, then." I headed toward the cabinet, intending to do some woodworking, but Hal stopped me.

"He should worship the ground you walk on, you know."

"What?"

"You heard me. Dylan doesn't appreciate you. I know about yesterday. I wasn't there, but sometimes space magic means I see and hear more than I should."

"It was beyond horrible, so I'm going to keep doing random acts of kindness for Dylan Khan if it's all the same to you."

"Are you sure you're okay with pining like Echo after Narcissus?"

"I'll live." I put my hand to my cheek.

He blinked, eyes reddening. Nin poked her head out of his pocket and squeaked, a series of shrill and angry sounds punctuated by an occasional click. Ember hung her head, giving me a reproachful stare.

"I'm sorry," I said, "I want you to live long and prosperously and have, like, ten kids with Faith."

"Me too. You aren't Echo. I just want to see you happy. Loved."

"Not everybody has someone destined for them, Hal. I'm okay with that."

Liar.

I didn't argue anymore with Hal or the Evil Inside Voice, but I didn't have the time or the heart to work on a carving of Dylan's dragonet either. I got a lump of clay and wedged it, preparing it for a piece to work on the next day instead.

In the magipsychic lab, we lucked out in the team department. I worked with Cadence, Izzy, Faith, and Brianna, which meant we could make those communication orbs.

Unfortunately, Professor Luciano wasn't our instructor. Instead, we were supervised by Principal Hawkins, Hal's neglectful mother. I didn't expect much, but she surprised me.

"I love this project." She smiled with genuine excitement. "Communication orbs were one of the first magipsychic items introduced to the mundanes after the Reveal, and they went a long way toward enabling us to integrate our societies."

"Miss, can we please just start?" Izzy had her hand up but didn't wait for an acknowledgment. She was excited, but Principal Hawkins had no idea.

"Part of the extramurals agreement was that we faculty members instruct as well as supervise. I chose this project myself, so I won't drop the ball, so to speak." She smiled, juggling three of the sea glass orbs we'd use in our project. "Don't worry, I know my stuff, and by the time you're done, so will you."

My knees went out from under me and I sat down hard, fortunately in my seat. Stephanie Hawkins' demeanor shocked me because it was nothing like Hal and Faith had described.

Faith sat there, silently wearing her best resting bitch face. I copied her, mostly in solidarity. Izzy joined in too, but Cadence acted like her usual bubbly self.

"I'm going to write some notes on this board here." She picked up a piece of chalk. "You ladies from Hawthorn already know, but I'll mention this for the other students. The booklets on the corner of your table automatically copy everything I put up, so there's no need for you to scribble. Just listen."

I'd learned most of the facts she lectured on by reading about communication orbs ahead of time, but Principal Hawkins was surprisingly entertaining. She gave us mnemonic devices disguised as quips, things we wouldn't soon forget, and when she demonstrated the tools and materials, she used techniques straight out of circus arts, as she had with the orbs.

Stephanie Hawkins was a natural teacher. Although all her extrahuman traits were passive, she understood the material and how we'd use it, and she conveyed it brilliantly. Even shifters were more magical than dhampyr, but nobody else seemed to mind. Especially not Brianna, who knew nothing about her true nature.

You see why Hal's father fell in love with her.

"Whatever." I winced immediately.

"I know, right." Faith elbowed me in the shoulder, briefly jostling Ember, who turned her head and went right back to sleep.

"All right, enough lecture. From now on, you'll have the entire lab period for the remainder of the week to collaborate on your project, write your report, and make your display. As an unassisted group, of course, though I'll be here for safety reasons. I can tell you guys are awesome, so rivals and frenemies might try to spy on you." She giggled. "Think of me more as security than a chaperone."

The work was more intensive than making three orbs with limited capabilities had been last year. This time we'd make six, with visual, audio, and recording capability. Each orb got coated with a mixture of infused solutions we made ourselves. These differences added loads of conjuring work, energy-charging, channeling, and chemical application.

Sorting the ingredients was a persnickety task. Some of the substances and items were nearly identical and stored in similar containers. Fortunately, Brianna had an eye for small details. We put her on the task of categorizing everything.

"I feel like a bull in a china shop here." Brianna stood with her hands behind her back. "It all looks so delicate, like if I sneezed, it'd break."

"Don't worry, we'll need your help with more than sorting." Cadence patted her shoulder. "Glamour is the key magic we'll use to enchant these."

"I'll help you," said Faith. "You point them out, I'll set them aside."

"Aliyah, I could use your help with these." Izzy beckoned me over.

She held a tray of unlabeled vials, all twelve containing white powder. Izzy needed my solar magic to tell them apart because six of them would temporarily turn purple when exposed to UV light. Sorting them must've taken longer than I thought because the bell rang before we knew it.

"See you guys tomorrow." Principal Hawkins opened the door, beaming and waving as we exited.

"Do you think we'll finish by the end of the week?" Brianna shook her head. "It seems impossible to get it done, and we still have Bishop's Row practice three nights a week."

"I'm on my school's team, so I know what you mean." I nodded. "We can totally do it, but we'll be tired."

"How do you think the others are doing?" Faith asked.

None of us knew, at least not until we got to dinner.

CHAPTER SIXTEEN

"Why do we have to be teammates, anyway?"

"Settle down." Lee got between Dylan and Dorian. "Professor Luciano picked you. Prove him right since he believes in you."

"You get along with everybody." Dylan snorted. "You've got no reason to be miserable."

"They separated me from my best friend." Lee shrugged. "Anyway, we've got to finish our project, and if we drop the ball, we're letting Grace, Keisha, and Azrael down. So let's get things under control long enough for that."

Dorian nodded. "He has a point."

"Shut your lazy mouth."

"Dylan, can you sit with me?" Logan picked at his thumbnail, one of the habits he couldn't shake in times of stress. "I've got questions about air magic, and the twins keep giggling and saying their ways are mysterious."

"You know everything anyway, but fine." Dylan followed Logan to a booth in the corner.

"He's moody." Izzy shook her head.

"Well, he's still upset over the whole thing."

"Yeah, I know. The breakup. But she's dated and dumped somebody entirely different since then. Is this much trauma normal for romantic people?"

"Well, how would you feel if you and Lee broke up?"

"I told you, we're best friends, not a couple."

"He's behind you."

"Yes, I am." Lee sidestepped to stand next to Izzy. "And she's right. We're not a couple. Anyway, everyone's different."

I couldn't tell them about the extramagus test, so I let them go on about relatively mundane stuff, puzzling things out between friendship and romance. Maybe I shouldn't have, but nobody has hindsight. Even precognitive psychics came by that selectively.

After that argument between Dorian and Dylan, we didn't see any more evidence of unrest from our year, but the first-years were another story. It started that night and got worse over time.

The first thing I noticed was Michelina Zanelli crying in the third-floor bathroom. Faith hadn't been in yet, and I was early for my soak in the clawfoot tub. It was a good thing, too. Michelina sat in one of the shower stalls, water running to wash away her tears as her opossum sat outside, whining miserably.

I waited until she was done and had some time to get dressed before approaching. Since I figured she wouldn't say much, I planned my words carefully.

"Hey, Lena. Welcome to the third-floor bathroom. You're welcome to use it anytime."

"Oh. Thanks, I guess." She pushed the curtain aside and emerged, hair still damp.

"Did you find everything okay? If you didn't, I could give you a little tour."

She nodded, then pointed at the wooden box of bath salts I held in my hand.

"All that stuff's in here."

I led Lena to the other side of the partition, showing her the wall panel where they stored a plethora of toiletries for tub baths. I took my time, explaining everything in my most neutral voice. Maybe she just needed space to calm down after whatever had sent her up here.

If she minded me over-explaining, Lena didn't show it. She followed me around as the toiletry explanation turned into a short tour. By the time we'd finished, she managed a hushed word of thanks before heading out of the bathroom.

Faith held the door for her as she left, then came in with a quizzical look on her face.

"What was that about?"

"I'm not sure. She was crying in there." I jerked my thumb at the shower. "Do you know who her roommate is? Could it be Temperance?"

"I'm not sure. All my sister and I have exchanged this year are dirty looks."

"Okay. Let's find out tomorrow."

"Good idea. Are you swimming tonight?"

"No, I'm too tired. I was just going to soak in one of the small tubs."

We each pursued our individual method of bathing. She was still swimming when I left for bed.

The next day was Friday, and I had to head home for the holiday. My family was preparing for Sukkot. The festival of booths was a lot of fun, even if we got rained out more often than not.

The point of the holiday was spending time with friends and family, so along with Cadence and Izzy, I also invited Dylan and Logan. Logan stayed behind once again, but Dylan left right after class with me, walking down Essex Street away from campus. He needed to escape campus even more than I did.

"Isn't Noah coming?"

"He'll be along later. Said something about extra library research for his group's project."

"Okay. What are we doing once we get there?"

"Mostly making decorations for the sukkah. Paper chains, popcorn on strings, woven fronds for the roof—that kind of thing."

"And then, if it doesn't rain, we have dinner there?"

"That's right."

"My mum would call that 'alfresco.'" He stared at the sidewalk. "Her favorite place to take holidays is in Italy.

"You must miss her."

"Yeah. I haven't seen her in over a year, Aliyah."

"I can't even imagine."

As we walked, I'd edged closer to him, so I dropped my hand beside his.

"I hope it stays that way for you."

He put some distance between us as we turned the corner on Hawthorne Street. We walked the rest of the way in silence, turning up the driveway behind Izzy's house toward 10-1/2. Around the back, we headed through the gate. The corner of the yard with the hole in the fence was currently occupied by a pile of lumber with canvas folded on top.

"That's it." I pointed.

"You only invited me so there'd be another tall person to hold those beams up, right?" He raised an eyebrow, but his eyes brightened.

"That might be among the many reasons, yes." I smiled, covering my hands' shaking. "Mostly I wanted to share a holiday with you. I know that sounds kind of sappy, but it's the truth."

"Right then." He cleared his throat. "How does this thing go together?"

"According to the instructions, of course." My dad stepped out from the back door, waving a piece of paper. "Which I happen to have right here."

Dad spent time with Dylan going over the directions, which weren't complicated. But my father believed in reading the manual. They took long enough that Noah finally showed up. Mom and Bubbe came out to the backyard, bringing a few critters to play in the exercise runs. After that, we all took part in setting up the sukkah.

Once we'd erected the frame, we took a break. Bubbe invited us in for iced tea. I helped her bring the critters back in, and we all stood around in her small kitchen with our beverages. She had a collection of arts and crafts supplies, which Noah, Dylan, and I worked with after the adults left the room with their tea.

"Are your holidays all kind of separated into the adults' table and the kids' table?"

"A little bit," said Noah. "It's more like they leave the fun stuff for us to do."

"Yeah, especially on Sukkot." I grinned, reaching for a container of glitter glue.

"It seems like a lot of work," Dylan said.

"It's a bit of a scramble before sundown, that's true." Noah nodded. "But we don't have to do anything after that besides hang out and eat."

"Will it be like Thanksgiving dinner again?" Dylan glanced over his shoulder at the oven behind him, his stomach growling.

"No, no turkey or any of that." I pointed at the oven. "But if my nose is not mistaken, Bubbe's got challah bread in there. We'll have that, along with some other dinner stuff."

"I wish Logan was here." Dylan sighed. "I feel like I've barely spent any time with him besides sleeping and getting ready for class in the morning."

Like you and Grace, but don't turn him into Gloomy McGloomypants by bringing her up.

"You guys are busy." Noah shrugged. "That happens in the second year. Everything's hectic for you guys, and extramurals are just another time sink."

"I asked Logan, but he doesn't want to leave campus. I think he's scared of his parents." I added a strip of glittery construction paper to a paper chain. "Azrael talked to his aunt. The Salem police won't bother him."

"Yeah, he knows." Dylan nodded. "But he's worried, almost paranoid. He has nightmares about them hiring people to cart him off to the airport."

Noah snorted. "That's ridiculous."

"It seems like that to us." It took a lot of effort not to snap at him. "But Logan's fear is valid. His parents are downright scary."

"Elanor's afraid of them too, but it's still ridiculous." Noah shook his head. "Not his feelings, the situation. I'll talk to him tomorrow. Maybe he'll come over in a large enough group. I know we're just students, but a throng of us can protect him from jerks in a van."

"That's a good idea." Dylan nodded. "This is done." He held up a paper chain. "What else should I make?"

"Whatever you want, I guess." Noah tapped a stack of brown paper. "How about guitars?"

"That's okay?"

"Yeah, we decorate with whatever's important to us that year." I nodded. "Last year, I put up a bunch of paper dragonets. I'd show you one, but they all got ruined in the rain."

He went to work cutting guitar shapes out of brown paper. The stove's timer buzzed, so I got up to take the bread out of the oven.

Moments later, Bubbe shooed us out of her kitchen. We'd finished enough decorations, so we went outside to help Dad put the fronds on top of the sukkah and hang our crafts on the walls inside.

After that, Noah and Dylan went upstairs. Through the window, we heard Noah singing along with Dylan's guitar. They played the same ten bars of music over and over with pauses in between, practicing a song I didn't recognize.

I helped get ready for dinner, but there wasn't much left to do. With most of the preparation done, all that remained was taking things out of ovens and letting them cool. The doorbell rang. Izzy and Cadence had brought Lee along with them.

As the sun set, we gathered in the backyard. Izzy and Cadence had seen all of this before, but Lee and Dylan hadn't.

"What's this one about?" Lee asked.

"We're celebrating how we survived in the wilderness after escaping Egypt," I answered. "This holiday lasts all week."

"Should be forty days since Moses got lost leading us around out there," Noah said.

"That's before he got those ten commandments, right?" Cadence said, "And before Google maps."

"You remembered." Noah grinned.

"So, now what?" asked Dylan.

134

"Mom and Dad are going to wave the four species, while Bubbe says a prayer."

"Four species? Is that like critters or something?" Lee raised an eyebrow. "How do you wave a mercat?"

"They're plants. We've got palm leaves, myrtle leaves, willow leaves, and citrus fruit."

"And after that, we can eat, I hope?" Dylan's stomach rumbled.

Everybody laughed. His smile reminded me of the ones on his face last year, definitely an improvement in his mood. Maybe music helped him cope or being off campus for a while did him good.

We all helped bring dinner downstairs. I had Bubbe's challah with raisins, dipped in honey. Also kreplach, stuffed dumplings like pierogis but with chicken instead of potatoes.

After dinner, Cadence and Izzy headed back to campus with Lee. Dylan lingered, bringing his guitar out and raising an eyebrow at Noah.

"Yeah, I think I'm ready to show it off." He went back inside and fetched his bass.

"Okay, one two three."

They did *Go Your Own Way* by Fleetwood Mac. Noah sounded like Lindsey Buckingham, too.

"You want to perform that in the talent show," Mom guessed.

"Something like that." Noah grinned. "It's not just us, though. Our band hasn't landed on the right song."

"That's awesome." I smiled.

"At least I'm not suspended from extracurriculars anymore." Dylan shrugged. "Only probation."

"Probation-smobation." Noah snorted.

"You're in the same boat as me." I nodded. "Plain old trouble." '

Mom picked up a stack of dirty dishes and started walking toward the house.

"Hey, I wanted to thank you guys for inviting me over. And everything else, too." Dylan stared down at the guitar. "I really needed some time away."

135

"Did you want to stay over?" asked Bubbe. "If you don't want to sleep out here, I've got space in my office."

"No, thanks. I've got to work before breakfast tomorrow." Dylan sighed. "Can't make my nights too late."

"Do you want me to walk you back?" Noah asked.

"No, I'll be all right. My feet know the way."

He packed the guitar into the library's battered case, and we escorted him through the gate together.

On warm enough nights, Noah and I slept in the sukkah. Because the New England weather was unpredictable, we got our sleeping bags. Mom and Dad said good night to us on our way out, but Bubbe sat outside on one of the folding chairs, staring at the stars.

"I'll get out of your way," she said.

We protested, letting her know she was welcome, but our grandmother must've had other things on her mind. She went inside after bidding us good night. We settled down in the Sukkah, moving the table and chairs and unrolling our sleeping bags in the newly cleared space.

I lay there, holding Great Uncle Noah's *Shema Yisrael* pendant between my fingers. It reminded me of the letters he'd written to his boyfriend, the ones Bubbe said I should share with Noah. I hadn't gotten a chance to look at them.

"Do you think we're in over our heads?" Noah stared at the fronds above his head.

"Absolutely, and we'll drown if we're not careful."

"Why?" He turned his head, so I did likewise to meet his gaze. "Just last week, you seemed the epitome of confident."

"If I tell you something, can you keep it secret? You might talk to Dylan about it, but nobody else."

"It's been ages since you've shared secrets with me, Aliyah. Sure. Go ahead."

I told him in vivid detail about the extramagus test. Probably I shouldn't have because the horror reflected on his face hit me like a sucker punch, but nobody can untell a story.

"So, that's why you fought so hard against Mom and Bubbe on Yom Kippur." He stared.

"Yeah." I closed my eyes, the tears I'd held back finally rolling down my face.

"I don't blame you, not one bit." He wiped them away.

"I'm sorry." I sniffled, opening my eyes.

"Why?" His face was blotchy, eyes bright.

"Neither of us will sleep well."

"Sleep's inevitable once you're tired enough." He sighed, gazing at the roof made of fronds. "I'm glad you told me. That's not the kind of thing to keep bottled up."

"I've learned that's how it is for extramagi—tucking all kinds of horrifying things into neat little boxes so we don't disturb anyone. Meanwhile, they're either jealous of our extra elements or afraid we'll go off the deep end."

"Aliyah, I'll never do the latter, but I'm guilty of the former." A gleaming line formed from the corner of his eye to one of his sideburns.

I couldn't decide how to respond. My brother's honesty wavered when it came to his shortcomings. Offering sympathy in this sukkah that symbolized nights spent in the wilderness was nothing short of miraculous to me.

There was one thing you could always say.

"Nobody's perfect. And thanks, Noah."

I don't know when he fell asleep because it was after I did. When I woke to the sun's first light and birdsong in the mulberry tree, he'd already left.

Before heading back to campus, I grabbed the box with Great-Uncle Noah's letters and tucked them into my backpack. I'd be more likely to read them if they were on campus with me.

CHAPTER SEVENTEEN

Our project progressed with little trouble. The others, not so much.

Hal's group worked on a magical toggle, something to turn lights off and on or open and close taps. He just barely managed to lead them via his knack for endearment. Having Bar on the team and backing his leadership helped, but the pair of snooty clairvoyants from Messing wasn't happy with his diminished magical ability. Kitty stuck up for him, but the clairvoyants dismissed her. Izzy said they thought she was "too mainstream," whatever that meant.

Lee, Dylan, Grace, and Azrael had to work with Dorian, who didn't contribute much. If it weren't for Lee and Keisha, the telepath from Messing, they wouldn't have kept the peace long enough to complete their refrigeration unit.

Noah worked with Elanor, Jonah, Crow, and Arick. They got along for the most part, though Crow's aloofness clashed with the otherwise gregarious crew. He also got distracted easily, and none of the others could keep him on task. Their project was one of the most demanding, a full-season carbon-free fuel for a magical space heater.

Logan's team technically had it easy with their magical water wheel, but they had to work with Alex and Temperance. Lena was in his group too, and Logan ended up doing most of the spellwork with her. The bear shifter and the telekinetic psychic on their team spent most of their time looking bewildered and lifting the heavy parts.

As the week drew to a close, we all scrambled. The devices were only one part of the projects. We'd have to compile data, write reports, and make everything in our display fit on top of a six-by-two foot table, so of course, everyone wanted the lab work done by Friday.

I crunched our numbers, and Brianna wrote all the text in the report. She had the best handwriting, like a scientist's. Despite her obvious ability, she had Cadence proofread it on Monday night.

"This is great work!" Cadence smiled.

"Thanks." Brianna grinned back.

"You just need to check the punctuation with someone else, because that's my weak point." She tapped an Oxford comma. "I'm not sure whether this should be here or not."

"I'll bring it to the library." I held my hand out for the notebook.

Brianna handed it over, turning to leave the lounge. Cadence cleared her throat and raised an eyebrow at her.

"Can I go with you?" Brianna asked.

"Sure, why not?"

We headed into the academic wing and down the hall. I was about to push the library doors open, but Brianna put her hand out, stopping me.

"Um, wait a minute." Her face was red and flushed as though we'd been at Bishop's Row practice instead of walking down a hallway.

"All right."

Eventually, she composed herself. Brianna took a deep breath and opened her mouth but closed it again and shook her head. Ember peeped at her from my shoulder.

Where have you seen this before, I wonder?

"Logan. Oops." I winced. "My inside voice jumps out sometimes."

"No, no, I understand. Are you two a thing?"

"We're not. He's got an enormous crush on someone else right now."

"Oh, okay then. Well."

"Well?"

"There's a dance. In December. The December Dance." She cleared her throat. "Do you have a date yet?"

"Oh!" I blinked. "Well, no. But, Bri—"

"So, do you want to go? With me, I mean. I won't be upset if you say no. Not everyone who's queer likes girls."

"I'm not sure if I'm queer, and I like you as a friend, but last time I had an actual date for something, it was a disaster."

"Well, maybe we should organize a stag group."

"Yeah, that'd be awesome. I bet Izzy would be down with that. Lee, too. And if Logan doesn't get his date..."

"Who's he asking?"

"He's probably hoping to get asked. Logan's super-awkward about stuff like that."

"Peep," Ember agreed.

"Me too, Ember." She laughed, her posture and expression more relaxed and easier than I'd seen in a while. "I guess it's library time."

She opened the door and we went inside, where all the grammar and style handbooks we could ever want waited for us.

That night, I walked into the cafeteria intending to chat with Logan and encourage him to ask Dorian to the dance, but he sidetracked me.

"Aliyah, have you heard anything about who poisoned Clementine?"

"What?"

"From Bubbe, I mean."

"No. She hasn't said anything."

"Have you asked her?"

"I haven't." I shook my head, the pit of my stomach dropping as my head got fuzzy and far away. "I feel horrible about it, too."

"You've had other things going on, what with getting pulled out of class and the holiday." He sighed. "But something new happened."

"Oh?"

"Yeah. Lena said she's afraid of getting in trouble about Clementine."

"So that's why she was crying." My hands curled into fists. "She was in the infirmary with us that afternoon. She couldn't have done it."

"Temperance is threatening her anyway. Said she'd get her expelled."

"Where are they?" I stood up.

"Not here." He grabbed my wrist. "Tempe left almost a half-hour ago, but Lena's in the corner with a book."

"I should talk to her." I pulled away and Logan looked past me, a pleading look in his eyes.

"Whoa there, Morgenstern." Dorian shook his head, stepping between me and the rest of the room.

"Sorry, Dorian. Gotta go."

"Not yet." He put a hand on my shoulder, as gentle and soft as the first snowflakes.

"It's important."

"Wait a minute." He sighed. "Please?"

"Okay." I waved at the empty chair beside Logan at the table and got back in my seat. "Step into our office."

Ember fluttered down to the table, peeping softly at Mercy and the gryphon cocked her head, shifting her weight from one foot to the other. Dorian ignored his familiar's discomfort. He turned the chair around and sat down, grinning. Logan nearly melted, but Dorian didn't notice. He stared at me.

Oh, no. Not another inconvenient admirer.

"What are your plans for the December Dance?"

He's smoother than the girl, at least.

Logan stood up and ran out of the cafeteria before I could do or say anything to stop him. Faster than he ever moved on the track in Gym, too.

"Dorian." I groaned. "He likes you, you idiot."

"What?"

"You heard me."

"Impossible. Logan's out of my league."

"Thanks."

"I didn't mean it that way. So, the dance?"

"I'm going stag." I pointed toward the door Logan left by. "Ask *him!*"

"Oh. Right!" Dorian got up and bolted.

I put my head down on my arms, unable to look at Logan's half-empty tray and my nearly full one. I'd clean them up, of course, but I just didn't have the heart at that moment. Ember peeped softly, then climbed on my back and settled against my neck.

"Aliyah Morgenstern?"

"If it's about the December Dance, I'm going stag," I mumbled.

"It's not."

I looked up too far because the person beside the table was almost as short as Hal had been last year. After lowering my gaze, I saw a boy with Dorian's coloring and high cheekbones, but he had a wiry sturdiness my friend did not possess. Then I recognized him.

"Cosmo. From the beach. You're the cat shifter with Blaine Harcourt."

"He wants to see you."

"Really?" I raised my eyebrow, skeptical.

At least it's not about the dance. Blaine's engaged.

"Yeah, really."

"I've got to do something first, though."

"Okay if I tag along?"

"Sure."

I stood up and carried the trays to the dishwashing window, then headed toward Lena with a confused Cosmo in tow. I sat across from her. Cosmo hovered by my elbow.

"Hi there." I let the corners of my mouth turn up but not too much. I didn't want to spook her.

"Hi." She blinked. Her opossum put her paws on the edge of the table and gave me an appraising look. "What is it?"

"I heard Tempe Fairbanks was giving you grief. How can I help?"

"There's nothing you can do since she's my roommate." Lena hung her head. "Why?"

"Because you shouldn't be bullied. You don't deserve that."

"Maybe I do. My element's poison. Clementine was poisoned."

"There's no way you did it."

"Are you sure?" She held the book up, partially obscuring her face. "Because I'm not. Every day she says I did it. That I'm the only person they didn't look at, and it's still unsolved, so it can only be me. Maybe she's right."

"Gaslighting," Cosmo chimed in.

"What?" I blinked.

"Gaslighting. My cousin Tony taught me all about it." He sat beside Lena and put his hand on the table, where she could see it. "The worst kinds of people do gaslighting. They mess with your head, so you don't know what's true."

The opossum sat up in Lena's lap. She leaned over the table, sniffed Cosmo's hand, then looked up at her magus and squeaked. Her fur glowed a faint purple.

"Yeah, Edie," she spoke to her familiar. "You were right."

"Should I have a chat with your roommate?" I asked.

"No." Behind the book, Lena shook her head. "I want out of that room."

"I'll work on that." I cleared my throat. "Also, I'm going stag to the December Dance in a group. You're welcome to join us."

"Really?"

"Yeah. My friends Lee and Izzy will be there. What do you think?"

"Okay."

"Awesome. We'll meet on the third floor by the stairs five minutes before it starts."

We said goodbye, and Cosmo and I left Lena to finish her dinner.

"You're that sure the headmaster will move her room?" he asked.

"Oh, yeah. I'll talk to Hal about it as soon as I've seen Blaine."

"Right, you're friends with his kid." Cosmo nodded. "Makes sense."

"Lead on, then."

Blaine was in the library, which was on extended hours for extramurals. Mrs. Ashford sat behind the desk, looking sleepy. That didn't stop her from giving me a friendly wave as Cosmo brought me to the back corner.

"Mr. Harcourt, you wanted to see me?"

"Yeah." He nodded. "It's about your friend Dorian Spanos."

"What about him?"

"Has he been acting unusual lately?"

"Are you trying to send him back to the Academy? Because if so, I'm leaving."

"No, never." Blaine put his hand over his mouth. "It's a horrible place. Kim still has nightmares about it."

"Okay. I'll do what I can, but he's not my best friend or anything."

"Well, that's sort of the problem."

I blinked.

"He's had trouble with that. Trusting people, I mean."

"Persuading me to buddy up with him won't help."

"It's not about friendship. He overheard something and kept quiet, largely because he doesn't know who to trust here."

"Why you?"

"Kim and I promised to help Dorian and his nephew Cosmo."

"Nephew!" I winced. "Oops."

"Yeah, it's a long and complicated story involving the Under."

"Okay." I nodded. "So, what's this thing Dorian heard?"

"It was about the poor familiar who got poisoned."

"You're telling me because my grandma examined the victim?"

"No. The people he overheard mentioned you."

Lovely.

I must have stayed silent too long for Blaine Harcourt's comfort since he resumed dropping bombs on me.

"Apparently, this duo, or perhaps an entire group, wants to remove all non-magi from campus, which I personally object to. They're willing to kill familiars over it, but first, they want to get rid of all the extramagi."

"All?" I blinked. "There are only two of us."

"The way Dorian put it, there's at least one more—someone with sealed records and influence here. Do you know who it is?"

"No."

"Perhaps Hal Hawkins?"

"Definitely not. He's got a medical condition, pernicious magiglobular anemia. That's the opposite of being an extramagus."

"Hmm." Blaine pulled out a phone that shouldn't have worked in here. Somehow, an app called LORA still functioned. He had a chat window open in seconds through it, with a series of fast replies after he entered what I'd just said. "Lynn says that means his mother's a dhampyr."

"Whoa." I shook my head. "That phone shouldn't work here."

"Yeah, I run with some real geniuses, and this app securely answers a ton of questions. Stuff we've been puzzled about for years."

"Does it have anything to do with why my uncle hasn't been sentenced yet?"

"Your uncle?" He raised an eyebrow.

"You didn't know?" I took a deep breath. "My mom's Richard Hopewell's little sister."

"Had no idea, but it makes sense, magically speaking." He nodded. "Listen, if it's okay with you, I'll tell Dorian to tell you his whole story."

"Go ahead." I nodded. "My grandma won't discuss Clementine, but my friends are trying to stop whoever did it from attacking again."

"We won't be in town much longer." He reached into his pocket, pulled out a card with a phone number on it, and handed it to me. "If you or your friends discover anything, would you mind keeping us informed? I think the connections between Newport and Salem are deeper than we imagined."

"When I'm off campus." I took the card. "I don't have a LORA."

"Right." He nodded. "Take your time, and thanks for meeting with me."

I left, baffled for the rest of the evening by how I could possibly be of any help to a dragon shifter chasing a Ph.D. I wouldn't figure that out until next year.

The story continues with book six, *Worthy Lives*, coming soon to Amazon and Kindle Unlimited

GLOSSARY

People

- **Changeling-** A mortal child of either one or two faerie parents. Most changelings choose a monarch sometime in their twenties, although some do it earlier than they have to.
- **Dampyr-** The mortal offspring of two vampires. They aren't as rare as many suspect, although because their blood is exceptionally sustaining to vampires, they keep their status secret. Dampyr sometimes have magic or psychic powers that work unreliably.
- **Faerie-** A term used to describe either a changeling who has tithed to a monarch and spent a year and a day in the Under or the pure creatures such as Gnomes and Pixies who were created by the king and queen.
- **Ghost-** A dead person with unfinished business becomes a ghost. If a mortal makes a contract before death, that gives them unfinished business and lets them linger. When ghosts finish their business, they move on, but no one knows where they go from here.

- **Magus**- A mortal who can use magic. Magic comes from energy in the world. Most magi can only use one type of magic. However, a rare few can do more than one kind. Those are called extramagi.
- **Merfolk**- People who can live on land with legs or in the sea with fins and tails. They only emerged from the ocean after the Big Reveal and are still extremely rare outside of harbor towns.
- **Psychic**- A mortal with psychic power. Psychic ability comes from a person's own body and mind.
- **Vampire**- An unliving person who drinks blood to survive and enhance their abilities. Only regular mortals, psychics, and magi can get turned into vampires. Shifters, changelings, and faeries won't turn, and most of those won't survive an attempt.
- **Shifter**- A mortal who can take an animal's shape. Shifters have one form, with coloring similar to what they have while human. They usually have an enhanced sense while human-shaped, which goes along with their animal. For example, an owl shifter might have keen eyesight and a wolf shifter, a great sense of smell.

Shifter Varieties

- **Dragon**- The only shifters who can see both magic and psychic abilities, though only while shifted. The most powerful ones can partially shapeshift. Dragons are immortal and reproduce infrequently. There are so few of them since the Reveal that they've started taking other magical shifters as mates.
- **Kelpie**- A magical shifter who gets their abilities from an enchanted faerie pelt that bonds with their soul. The Kelpie pelts were created by the Goblin King, so they have Unseelie energy and restrictions. A Kelpie's animal form is a horse. Families pass the pelts down through generations,

and part of each ancestor lives on to help their descendants. The ancestors can get distracting, however.

- **Selkie**- A magical shifter who gets their abilities from an enchanted faerie pelt that bonds with their soul. The Selkie pelts were created by the Sidhe queen, so they have Seelie energy and restrictions. A Selkie's animal form is a seal or sometimes a sea otter. They can use water magic as long as they wear the pelt. Families pass the pelts down through the generations, and part of each ancestor lives on to help their descendants. The ancestors can get distracting, however.
- **Tanuki**- A magical shifter with enhanced speed and the ability to see all types of magic while shifted. They are also the only creatures who can manipulate luck, causing it to turn from good to bad or the other way around. They stop aging if they own a charm infused with luck from humans. Very few of those charms exist, having been either used up during the Reveal or locked away.

Powers

- **Air magic**- The power to conjure, control, and banish wind or air.
- **Earth magic**- The power to conjure, control, and banish earth, sand, or rock.
- **Empathy**- A psychic power to sense and influence emotions in other people.
- **Fire magic**- The power to conjure, control, and banish flames.
- **Ice magic**- The power to conjure, control, and banish ice.
- **Lightning magic**- The power to conjure, control, and banish lightning.
- **Poison magic**- The power to conjure, control, and banish poison. Each magus has a slightly different type of toxin they produce. Some are even antidotes to others.
- **Precognitive**- A psychic power to foretell future events.

- **Spectral magic**- the power to conjure, control, and banish light.
- **Spectral Affinity**- A trait some spectral magi have that makes them charismatic and believable.
- **Summoner**- A psychic power that lets the user make contracts with pure faeries, letting the summoner call them in times of need. Each creature has an anchor, some item symbolizing the bond. Mastery of summoning takes decades of study, which is why the most powerful are either vampires or past middle age.
- **Seelie**- The Sidhe queen's court. The Seelie way is about following the letter of the law, even when it's hard or cruel. They have a hard time reconciling faerie rules with the new mortal laws since the Big Reveal.
- **Solar Magic**- The power to conjure, control, or banish sunlight. Some of the most powerful practitioners can find hidden objects or discover long-kept secrets.
- **Solar Affinity**- A trait some solar magi have that makes them beacons for coincidence.
- **Space magic**- The power to move the self or objects instantly across distances. Some can even move other people.
- **Space Affinity**- This space power comes with an ability to locate people or things important to the magus.
- **Telekinesis**- A psychic power that moves objects.
- **Telepathy**- A psychic power to read minds.
- **Tithe**- The process of pledging to either the queen or king, making a changeling choose to be either Seelie or Unseelie.
- **Umbral magic**- The power to conjure, control, and banish shadows and veil or camouflage objects or people.
- **Umbral Affinity**- A trait some umbral magi have that makes them difficult to remember without psychic ability, faerie magic, or a shifter pack bond.
- **Undeath magic**- The power to conjure, control, and banish unliving energy.

- **Unseelie**- The Goblin king's court. The Unseelies bend the rules and often navigate mortal society more easily than their Seelie counterparts.
- **Water magic**- The power to conjure, banish, and control water.
- **Wood magic**- The power to conjure, banish, and control wood. It takes extreme power to influencing a living plant.

Creatures

- **Basilisk**- A venomous serpent that also has poison magic.
- **Dragonet**- A tiny dragon-like creature, always associated with one or more element which powers their breath attacks later in life. They have scales but are warm-blooded like birds. Most don't get much bigger than a small cat.
- **Familiar**- A magical or mythical creature who makes a bond with a magus.
- **Gryphon**- A chimera which has the head of a bird and hindquarters of a predatory mammal. They come in several combinations of base species, and habitat influences their choice in magi to bond with.
- **Karkus**- A crab that can change its shape. They're said to be the offspring of the crab that pinched Hercules as he battled the Hydra.
- **Lightning Bird**- A familiar from South Africa with an affinity for lightning. Its beak can jump-start a car.
- **Mercat**- A shapeshifting feline with fur for land and scales in the water. They can live in lakes, rivers, or in the sea as well as on land. They must never completely dry out, or they will die.
- **Moon Hare**- A magical rabbit that gets power from its particular moon phase. They commonly bond with umbral magi.
- **Pharaoh's Rat**- These natural predators of dragon shifters are the size of ferrets and resemble a mongoose with more

fur. They have an affinity for space magic and can use it on occasion.

- **Pigeon**- Not as mundane as most think, some pigeons have an uncanny sense of direction due to their affinity for air magic.
- **Pricus**- An aquatic goat said to be descended from Capricorn. They can warp time even better than Gnomes.
- **Pure Faeries**- Creatures who spring to life from magical sources in the Under. They are genderless, and their type and ability depend on place of origin. They're associated with only one court, although they will work together to defeat a common enemy.
- **Sand Cat**- A feline that lives in the desert, able to go for weeks without water. Earth magic lets them do this.
- **Sha**- A magical desert dog from Egypt. Sha are the size of mundane toy breeds with short hair and small pointy ears. They could pass for mundane except for their blue tongues. They are attracted to anything undead.
- **Sphinx**- A magic cat with an affinity for fire. The reason they're hairless is that they're resistant to flames.
- **Strix**- A venomous owl with an affinity for poison. Female striges have rounded tufts on their heads, while males have pointed ones.
- **Sumxu**- A lop-eared cat found only in northern China. They are masters of camouflage and have an affinity for several kinds of magic.

Places

- **The Academy**—Something between a community college and a military academy for extrahumans, the Academy is geared toward helping extrahumans who don't play well with mortals get ready to join a blended society. It's got divisions for learners of all ages, though they are housed separately.

- **Cherry Blossom School**- A dojo geared toward teaching extrahumans self-restraint, meditation, and how to temper their enhanced physical abilities with more mundane skills. It's been around for close to a hundred years, run by the Ichiro family. Mundane classes used to be offered as a front but now are a separate division.
- **Ellicot City Magitechnic**- A prep school for magi and psychics specializing in magipsychic technology. It's located outside Baltimore.
- **Gallows Hill School**- Traditionally for shifters, this prep school in Salem recently opened its doors to changelings and other extrahumans not categorized as magi or psychics.
- **Hawthorn Academy**- A preparatory school for magi in Salem. Its campus is in the space between the mortal realm and the Under, giving it unrivaled privacy. They specialize in teaching familiar magic.
- **Providence Paranormal College**- A school founded just one year after Brown University and located right in its shadow. Providence Paranormal used to admit only magi and psychics, but it's been accepting all types of extrahumans ever since Henrietta Thurston became headmistress. There has been trouble since then for students and faculty, leading people to believe dissenters are sabotaging the school.
- **Trout Academy**- A prestigious preparatory school for changelings with magic, recently open to magi and magical shifters. Its campus is located in South County and has been operating in some form or another since Rhode Island Colony was founded.
- **The Under**- The faerie realm. It's been divided into two parts ever since the Sidhe Queen and the Goblin king split up thousands of years ago. Mortals don't age in the Under, but it's a dangerous place for them to be. Getting lost means never being seen again, and it's easy to get indebted to

something nasty while trying to get through or out of the Under.
- **Wolf Messing Prep**- An institute for psychics to learn to control their skills before heading to college.

Events

- **The Big Reveal**- The term used for the 1990s, when the world discovered magic was real and extrahumans existed. The decade was marked with fear as everyone adjusted to the changes. Since the 21st Century, law and technology work for both humans and extrahumans.
- **Boston Internment**- A reaction by Boston government officials to the disappearance and suspected trafficking in extrahumans, especially shifters. All registered extrahumans in Boston lived on barges for close to a month under guard by the Boston Police. The traffickers got their hands on some magical gadgets, rendering the protection useless. Few survived.

THANK YOU!

Thank you for reading! If you loved this book, please leave a review. You can find my other work by clicking the links below, going to **my website** or visiting my **Author Central page**.

ALSO BY D.R. PERRY

Providence Paranormal College

Bearly Awake (Book 1)

Fangs for the Memories (Book 2)

Of Wolf and Peace (Book 3)

Dragon My Heart Around (Book 4)

Djinn and Bear It (Book 5)

Roundtable Redcap (Book 6)

Better Off Undead (Book 7)

Ghost of a Chance (Book 8)

Nine Lives (Book 9)

Fan or Fan Knot (Book 10)

Hawthorn Academy

Familiar Strangers (Book 1)

Acting in Kindness (Book 2)

Fire of Justice (Book 3)

Learning to Give (Book 4)

Light of Equality (Book 5)

Gallows Hill Academy

Year One: Sorrow and Joy (Book one)

For other books by DR Perry please see her Amazon author page.

CONNECT WITH THE AUTHOR

Website: https://www.drperryauthor.com/

Join her newsletter!

Find more of D.R. Perry's books on Amazon.

OTHER LMBPN PUBLISHING BOOKS

To be notified of new releases and special promotions from LMBPN publishing, please join our email list:

http://lmbpn.com/email/

For a complete list of books published by LMBPN please visit the following pages:

https://lmbpn.com/books-by-lmbpn-publishing/

www.ingramcontent.com/pod-product-compliance
Lightning Source LLC
Chambersburg PA
CBHW050401110726
47899CB00008B/2607